# FLY ON THE WALL

Remy Lai

HENRY HOLT AND COMPANY • NEW YORK

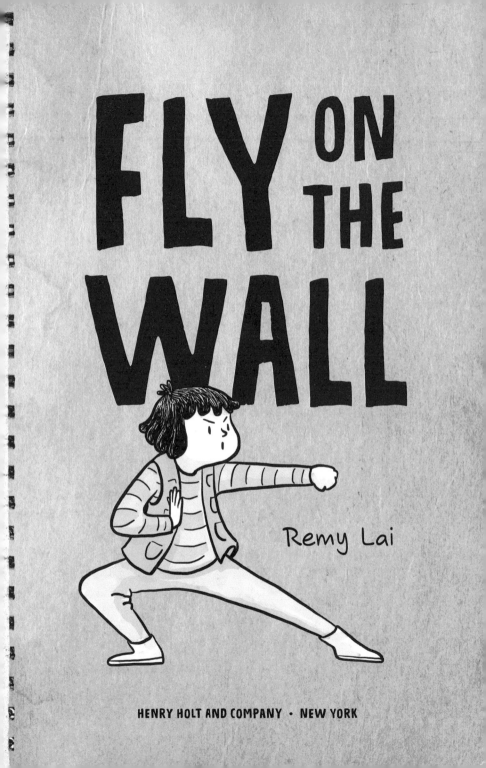

Henry Holt and Company, *Publishers since 1866*

Henry Holt® is a registered trademark of Macmillan Publishing Group, LLC

120 Broadway, New York, NY 10271 · mackids.com

Library of Congress Control Number: 2019949491

ISBN 978-1-250-31411-6

Our books may be purchased in bulk for
promotional, educational, or business use. Please
contact your local bookseller or the Macmillan
Corporate and Premium Sales Department
at (800) 221-7945 ext. 5442 or by email at
MacmillanSpecialMarkets@macmillan.com.

First edition, 2020 / Designed by Carol Ly

Colors by MJ Robinson

Printed in the United States of America by LSC
Communications, Crawfordsville, Indiana

10  9  8  7  6  5  4  3  2  1

"TOOT!"

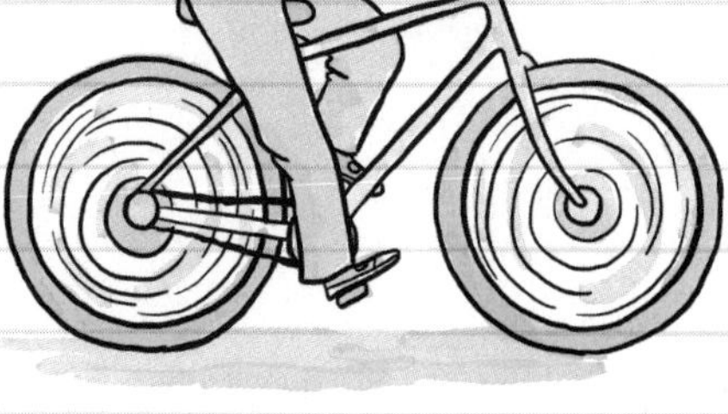

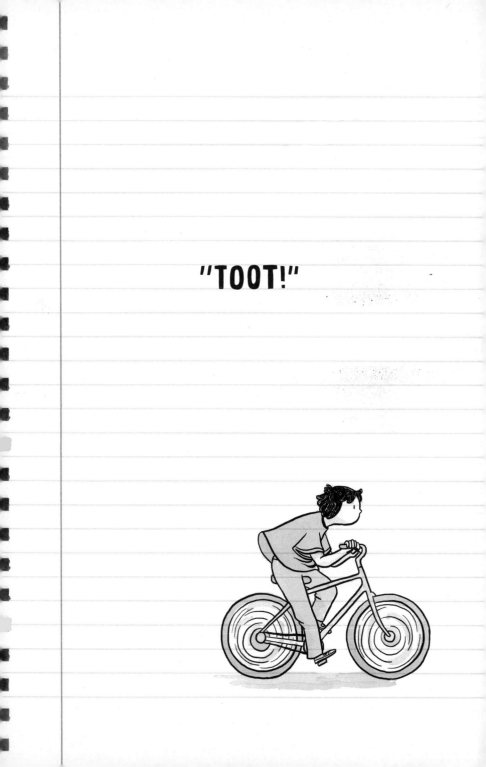

THIS BOOK BELONGS TO
# HENRY KHOO

PRIVATE!

KEEP OUT!

If found, please return to
henrykhoo@geemail.com

1

The night before the greatest adventure everrr
In my bedroom

The greatest adventure everrr isn't just not allowed. It's FORBIDDEN. Like, Entry into this Radioactive Building is FORBIDDEN.

In my case, it's: Twelve-year-old is FORBIDDEN from Flying Halfway Across the World on His Own.

It's also: Twelve-year-old is FORBIDDEN from Doing Anything on His Own Because His Family Thinks He's a WAH-WAH-WAH Baby.

Do not copy this plan, fellow kids!

I'll be like the lone wanderer in my grandma's martial arts TV dramas. Popo isn't an actor; she just yells at the wuxia actors on the screen from her ancient, squishy armchair.

As the lone wanderer, I'll traverse the lands and face dangerous trials and tribulations.

The lone wanderer usually

travels on foot or horseback, because wuxia dramas always take place in the time before Toyotas and Jeeps. But I'll be on an airplane.

I'll meet a martial arts master.

Be my disciple. As your shifu, I'll impart my wisdom to you.

Shifu!

Teach me how to fix everything that's wrong in my life.

And me.

I will star in a montage showing off all my hard work.

Huff!

Hi-ya!

Puff!

I'll run into my nemesis during my journey, and we'll face off in a final duel. At first, I'll be losing. But just when you think I'm bye-bye, I'll spring to my feet and . . .

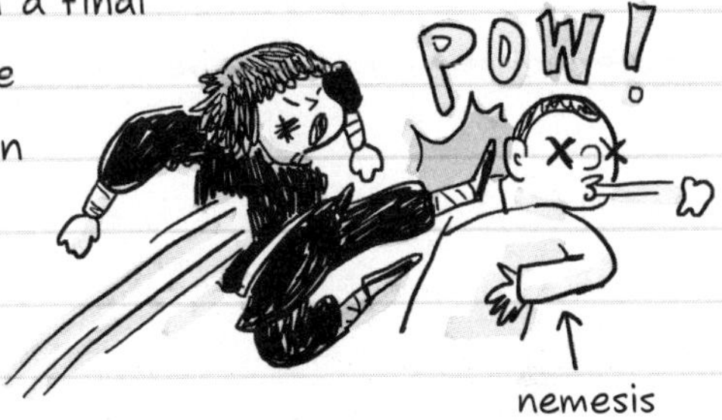
POW!
nemesis

But before THE END, I'll do something kind.

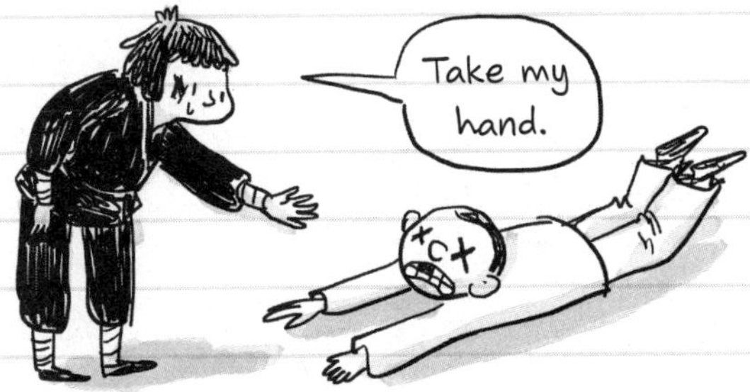
Take my hand.

That will prove I've gained wisdom that's much, much deeper than

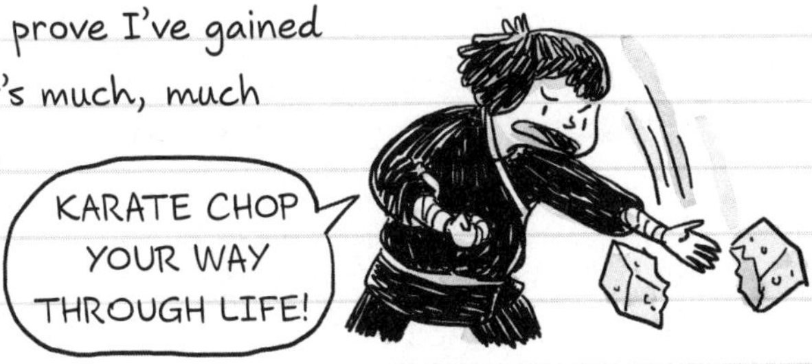
KARATE CHOP YOUR WAY THROUGH LIFE!

Of course, all good wuxia dramas have something else . . .

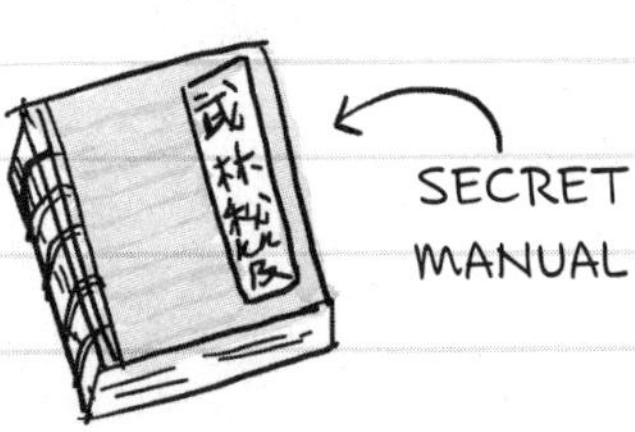
SECRET MANUAL

It's an old book fought over by everyone in the wuxia world, where wanderers stride, nemeses hide, shifus guide, sworn brothers confide, kicks and fists slide, and evil and justice collide.

Within the pages of a secret manual is life-changing wisdom, such as the steps of an ancient technique to POW! your nemesis. Similarly, my notebook will contain all the knowledge Mom keeps promising I'll have when I'm older, like the words to WOW! more friends.

I'll reach my destination in victory. I'll make an international call back to my family in Perth, Australia, and ask to be put on speakerphone.

If you're a grown-up, why
are you still
reading
this?
Not that I have anything against grown-ups.
But you might think it's not a big deal
to be treated like a baby.
That it's not worth this much trouble.
That it's not worth traveling halfway across the
world for.

If you're a kid,
you'll understand.

There was once a boy
of medium height, medium weight, medium IQ,
medium handsomeness, medium everything.
So unremarkable is he
that his middle name is Meh.

The only remarkable thing about him is
his crying.

He does it a bit more often than other kids do.
But that's not a thing you want a trophy for, is it?

One fateful day last December,
his sister dragged and dumped him
at an after-school program,
Poetry for Kids.
He was a baby
who had to do as he was ordered.
The dictator-poet-teacher said, *Create poems!*
But all this kid's poems
turned out to be meh,
just like this one.

If you ever knew a kid
who felt as meh
as this kid,
you'd understand
why he needs this
victory.

## COUNTDOWN TO FLIGHT

`0` `3` `4` `5`

**HOURS**    **MINUTES**

First day of school break, day of the greatest
adventure everrr
Dining room, Henry Khoo's home

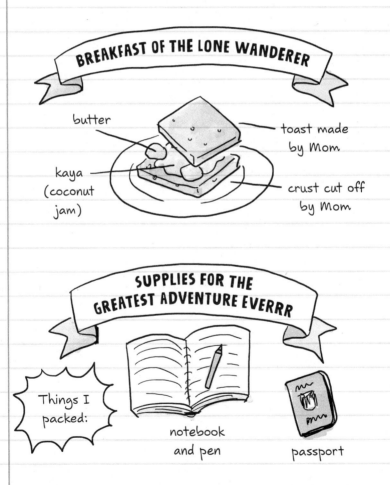

**BREAKFAST OF THE LONE WANDERER**

butter

kaya
(coconut
jam)

toast made
by Mom

crust cut off
by Mom

**SUPPLIES FOR THE
GREATEST ADVENTURE EVERRR**

Things I
packed:

notebook
and pen

passport

SUPPLIES FOR THE GREATEST ADVENTURE EVERRR (CONTINUED)

Things my family stuffed in my bag for where they think I'm going (to Pheebs's house, a two minute drive away):

first aid kit

sunscreen

spare underwear

umbrella

poncho

sweater

muesli bar

bottle of water

chrysanthemum tea drink

chocolate milk

hat

hand sanitizer

Since the greatest adventure everrr is top secret, I cooked up an alibi and told my family I'm spending the day at my best friend forever Pheebs's house. My BFF and I will supposedly be completing a school project with six other classmates.

Where I'm really going is two thousand five hundred miles away, across an ocean and a sea, to Dad's apartment in Singapore.

Dad lives in Singapore, a little island on the equator.

My mom, grandma, sister, and I live in Perth, a big blob on Australia.

Thanks to Popo, Mom, and Jie, Dad thinks I'm a baby. We stay with him every school break. Whenever the others are fussing over me, Dad glances up from his newspaper and says, "Henry, you can make your own toast, can't you?" or "Henry, you don't have to be reminded to take a shower, do you?" or "Henry, you can blow on your own soup, can't you?"

But I still like Dad, because he's quiet like me.

In Perth, whenever Popo, Mom, and Jie are

yakking their heads off, I think of that test I used to do in second grade.

**IN EACH GROUP, CIRCLE THE THING THAT DOESN'T BELONG.**

I'm the broccoli, the book, the mushroom. But Dad's also the broccoli, the book, and the mushroom. And it's much better to not be odd alone.

Singapore is the one place where my older sister is as friendless as I am. There, Jie has zero right to tell me, "Oh, Henry, you should listen to all the *buts* your teachers write on your report cards every year." But *Henry should learn to be more articulate, to speak up more.* But *Henry should participate more.* But *Henry needs to make more friends.*

For the past few months, ants had been crawling in my pants as I waited for school to end. I could not wait to fly off to Singapore again. But one morning last month, I shuffled into the kitchen in my PJ's and . . .

Turned out, I'd missed the meeting where my family decided that we wouldn't be making the usual five-hour-and-fifteen-minute flight to Singapore. Turned out, this meeting had been conveniently held after the bedtime they set for me.

I interrupted their sharing of plans.

I can go visit Dad by myself.

Everyone fell silent and stared at me. Even Maomi's tail froze mid-wag. I knew my words could stop conversations, but I had no idea they could stop time.

Then Maomi huffed through his nose. He probably didn't think my superpower was cool, since it had nothing to do with conjuring liver snaps out of thin air. His disappointed huff restarted time and dialed my family's volume up to a hundred.

YOU'LL CATCH A COLD! YOU'LL GET LOST!

那我得跟谁看武侠剧啊? 猫咪? (Who will I watch wuxia dramas with? Maomi?)

YOU'LL CRY! YOU'LL GET HURT! YOU'LL GET KIDNAPPED! BLAH BLAH BLAH BLAH BLAH

My family's predictions of what would happen if I got a taste of freedom, a.k.a. Consequences of Henry Khoo's Jailbreak, closed in on me. I felt something I'd never felt before, like . . .

I'd rather not overflow or Pop! or BOOM!

To stop myself from exploding, that night I came up with The Plan.

THE PLAN

7:33 AM
Leave my house (Jie is driving me)

7:35 AM
Arrive at Pheebs's house

Jie interrogates my alibi

7:45 AM
Jie leaves and I hail a taxi on my own

Get through airport security

8:15 AM
Arrive at Perth airport

10:45 AM
FLIGHT TAKES OFF!

4:00 PM
Land at Singapore airport

4:30 PM
Hail a taxi

Get through customs

4:45 PM
Arrive at Dad's apartment

THE CALL

5:00 PM
My family is supposed to pick me up from Pheebs's house

Since the drive from my house to Pheebs's house takes two minutes, to catch Mom and Jie before they leave to pick me up from Pheebs's, I have to reach Dad's apartment and call home by 4:55 PM.

The time is now 7:30 AM, and I've just finished my crustless toast. I'm right on time.

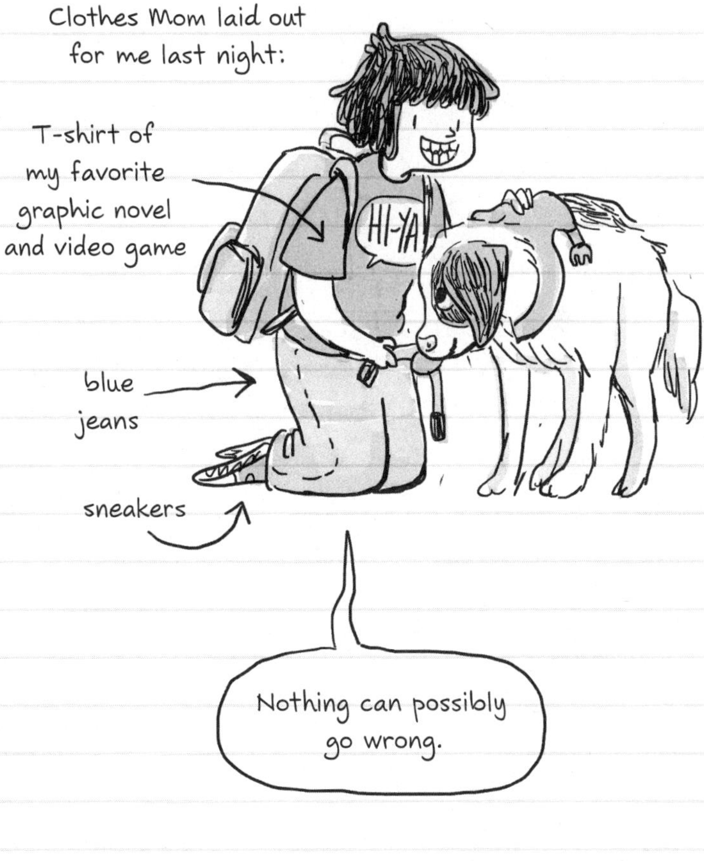

Clothes Mom laid out for me last night:
T-shirt of my favorite graphic novel and video game
HI-YA
blue jeans
sneakers
Nothing can possibly go wrong.

Driveway of Henry Khoo's house
23 minutes behind the schedule in The Plan

One of the things that stinks about being twelve is
you're old enough to plan things on your own, but
whether your plan is a success or a flop depends on
the grown-up with a driver's license. That's why there
are no twelve-year-old supervillains. They'd have to wait
for the grown-up to finish their older-people business
before the kid supervillain could catch a ride to the
secret villain headquarters. If the grown-up was too
busy, the kid supervillain would have to reschedule
their MUAHAHAs for another time. What a bummer.

In my case, The Plan now hinges on Jie. She
should be in our Toyota, driving me to Pheebs's house,
but she's still in the bathroom. What a bummer.

It's only the start
of the adventure, and
The Plan already needs
an ambulance.

I don't know what made me think I could pull

this off. I've never done a solo adventure. I've never even done *just* adventure or *just* solo.

At thirty minutes behind schedule, a warmth spreads behind my nose. That's a sign that I'm about to cry. Which would be the exact opposite of proving that I'm not a baby. Luckily, a second later, Jie climbs into our car, jolting The Plan back to life.

"Whatchu writing in that book?" she asks.

I brush aside the tiny bits of whitish nail that are littered on my notebook like dandruff. "Private."

Jie guffaws. At least that's what I think it is. I read about people guffawing in books, but I don't exactly know how you guffaw. "Private? Where did you even learn that word? I know everything about you. I've seen your wee-wee when we changed your diapers. I've even seen that poop-shaped birthmark on your back that you've never seen. Private? Oh, Bao Bao!"

*Ugh.* That nickname.

In Mandarin, a bun is called a bao, but a bao bao is not bun-bun or two buns or a butt.

It's very confusing. Welcome to my life and my twice-weekly Mandarin lessons with Popo.

The strange thing is, Jie has been calling me Bao Bao since forever. It never used to bother me. But at some point recently, I don't know how or why, when I wasn't paying attention, things changed. Maybe it all started when I turned eleven and no owl dropped by with a letter that said I was actually a wizard and very special. Now, being called Bao Bao makes me want to:

But we're reversing out of the driveway, and opening the door of a moving car is dangerous. Plus, I don't have a pillow. I do something else instead:

News flash: Slamming a book is as satisfying as eating only a single candy from your Halloween loot.

"Bao Bao," Jie says, completely ignoring my book slamming, "are you excited about spending the day with your classmates? Making new friends?"

"Of course!" I swivel my head around and look at Maomi. I can't let Jie see my face or she'd know I'm lying.

"Maomi! That's poison!" Jie says. "You've been really gassy lately. Fart once more, and I'll send you to the pound."

Telepathically, I thank Maomi for his fart. The stink distracts Jie from seeing the flame engulfing my LL-sized pants. LL for Liar Liar. To go on the greatest adventure everrr, I've told a million lies. I'll be telling another gazillion.

It's not that I'm a Goody Two-shoes. I've worn one shoe many times and lied about little things, like telling

Jie that her loofah had dog fur all stuck in it because Maomi was shedding for summer and that was the only reason his fur was everywhere. She'd then said, "Maomi, stop shedding, or I'll send you to the pound."

It wouldn't do her any good to know that I'd simply decided to give Maomi an extra-sudsy bath.

But those little unplanned lies are different from the million lies I've been telling the past few weeks, because I plotted these in advance. I spied on Jie online-shopping for clothes and makeup. I had to do that several times before all those numbers on Mom's credit card were stored in my brain.

I even had to pretend to agree with Jie that cherry, crimson, and rose are different colors. When I'd first told her that her three brand-new sweaters looked the same, she saw red. Or did she see crimson?

Then I went online. A few clicks, and I'd bought a plane ticket to Singapore. By the way, I'm not a thief; I paid Mom back for my ticket by adding $152.99 to the emergency cash stash Mom keeps in her wardrobe, in the right pocket of the seventh coat from the left.

Finally, this morning, after Mom left for the

farmers' market, I asked Popo, "你可以把我的护照给我吗？我要用来做作业。" (May I have my passport? It's for a school project.)

Popo didn't ask what kind of school project required a passport. She didn't ask anything, because she doesn't get how school projects work. Or internet or Netflix. Right after handing me my passport, she went back to watching her wuxia dramas, which are stored in shiny plates from the Mesozoic era called DVDs—Discs Viewed by Dinosaurs.

"Henry," Jie says, interrupting my thoughts, "did you pee before we left?"

"I'm twelve! I think I can hold it. And I might be wrong, but I think there's probably a bathroom at Pheebs's house. I hear most houses have them."

"Sarcasm is not your forte. Did you pee or not?"

"Yesyesyesyes!" That's another lie, but you see how my family lights my pants on fire? They'd never have let a bao bao go on an international adventure. They believe I'm spending half a day at my classmate's house, and they act like I signed up to be a:

RACE CAR DRIVER!

. . . who has a part-
time job as an . . .

ASTRONAUT!

YUM
YUM!

. . . with a mission to explore
a planet inhabited by aliens
whose number one snack food is kids.

"There she is," Jie says as we pull into my alibi
and classmate's driveway. "Your BFF."

I gulp. I've been lying to my family about Pheebs
too. Not just the part where I'm not actually going
to be spending the day at her house.

My family has
no idea that for
the past half
a year . . .

. . . Pheebs hasn't been my BFF.
She's been my NRFF. Not Really Friend Forever.

Our car is turning into Pheebs's driveway

HI-YA!

Pheebs is at her front porch. She's wearing the same T-shirt as I am. It's from the graphic-novel-turned-video-game that we used to play together. Before our friendship was Game Over.

Actually, Pheebs and I have many of the same T-shirts. That's how close we used to be.

Our friendship happened when Pheebs transferred into my school in the middle of first grade. She was walking down the rows of tables looking for a place to sit when I put up my hand and said she could sit next to me. We just fit together, like fish and chips, like icy pops and summer days, like porridge and Popo's dentures. In no time, we became BFFs.

When we were little, we pretended we were characters in Popo's wuxia dramas.

From this day on, we are sworn siblings.

We will be loyal to each other forever.

chrysanthemum tea drink

Except the *HI-YA!* T-shirt now reminds me how we're no longer sworn siblings. Since grown-ups like to say *time heals all wounds*, I've been hoping that somehow Pheebs and I could be friends again, but the only reason she agreed to be my alibi today is because I bribed her—in exchange, she gets a day with Maomi. She didn't even ask what I was actually up to.

When Pheebs first came into my life, she immediately joined Jie in begging Mom for a dog, and finally, three years ago, instead of *maybe*, *we'll see*, or *next year*, Mom said, "Pick a breed." Pheebs loves Maomi so much that every school break, she insists he stay with her while my family is in Singapore.

It feels strange that she's in the dark about this momentous adventure. We've shared everything else—

losing baby teeth, sprouting adult teeth, growing tall enough to reach the diary Jie hides in her wardrobe, and getting scolded by Jie for reading the diary in her wardrobe. But I can't bring myself to tell Pheebs about The Plan. One, I'm afraid she might tattle. Two, I'm afraid she might think I'm being a baby about being treated like a baby. Reason number three, the one I'm most afraid of, is how she might . . .

I open the passenger door. Maomi wags his tail so hard I worry his butt might fall off. He can't wait to get cuddles from Pheebs.

As I unbuckle him out of the car, Jie transforms.

Pheebs is so close to my family that, like me, she doesn't call my sister by her name.

"Jie!" I step in between them. "Don't you have somewhere else to be?"

Jie waves me off like I'm an annoying fly. "Keep writing in your private book and don't interrupt me. Pheebs, where are the other group members? There are six of them, right?"

Calmly, Pheebs scratches Maomi behind his ears. She's used to Jie's interrogation. "Dad is out, and Pa is in the bathroom. Our six other classmates are arriving a little later." Pheebs can even predict what the next interrogation questions will be: She adds, "For lunch, we're ordering pizza. For snacks, we have an unlimited supply of muffins, celery sticks, and chopped-up fruit."

"Pizza" makes a smile break out on Jie's grumpy detective face. Mom only allows us to eat pizza if we happen to be out. If we're home, the only meals we'll have are home-cooked meals. When Pheebs used to come to our house, Jie and I would make her tell Mom that she wanted pizza. Since Mom thinks being a good host is important, she always agreed.

But pizza doesn't make me smile anymore. They served pizza at Pheebs's birthday party half a year ago.

The party that I ruined.

Last December, my family and I came home

from our trip to Singapore three weeks early
because Jie had a group project to complete. As our
taxi pulled up our driveway, Pheebs happened to be
cycling past with two other classmates.

Austin Turner

Deepal Shah

I thought then that Pheebs's surprised reaction
was the good kind of surprised.

Dee spoke first: "Henry, are you going to
Pheebs's birthday party tomorrow?"

I turned to Pheebs. "Tomorrow is your birthday?"

"I didn't tell you about the party because I
thought you wouldn't be around."

That was the first time I'd ever thought about
Pheebs's birthday. In my defense, it was the first
time I was ever around on her birthday, and in my
family, birthdays aren't a big deal. Popo or Mom cooks
the birthday person's favorite food. That's it. The only
presents I get are from Pheebs, usually a bag of candy.

"Are you going, Henry?" Dee asked.

"Of course," I said. "It's Pheebs's birthday."

If only I could turn back time. I'd have said I had a doctor's appointment for an extra-contagious cold virus that makes the patient get the cold shoulder from everyone else.

Jie pats my backpack, tapping me out of my memories. "There's a first aid kit in here," she says. "Pheebs, your pa's first aid certificate is still valid, right?"

Pheebs smiles. "Pa just got off his ambulance shift, so I'd say yes."

Jie nods like she's satisfied.

## JIE THE CLUELESS DETECTIVE

Jie, Jie, Jie,
Now you stand akimbo
on the porch of my NRFF,
and shoot questions
and yammer on
Henry can't have prawns,
Henry has to apply suntan lotion,
Henry is such a delicate flower.
If something happens to Henry,
I will bring about the apocalypse.

Like you know everything about me.
But little do you know,
the reason Pheebs hasn't been coming over to our house,
the reason I haven't been going over to hers,
has nothing to do with her failing grades
or her having to study after school
like I told you.
The fact is, Pheebs gets all A's
and there are no *buts* in her report cards.

Jie, Jie, Jie,
There are things you don't know about Pheebs.
You look at her
and the way
she doesn't roll
her eyes. You
can't see the
knives hidden
behind her
Colgate smile.
Jie, you forget,
Pheebs is called a wolf in sheep's clothing
by the anonymous, mysterious
Fly on the Wall.

# FLY ON THE WALL

**WOLF STALKS CHATSWOOD SCHOOL**

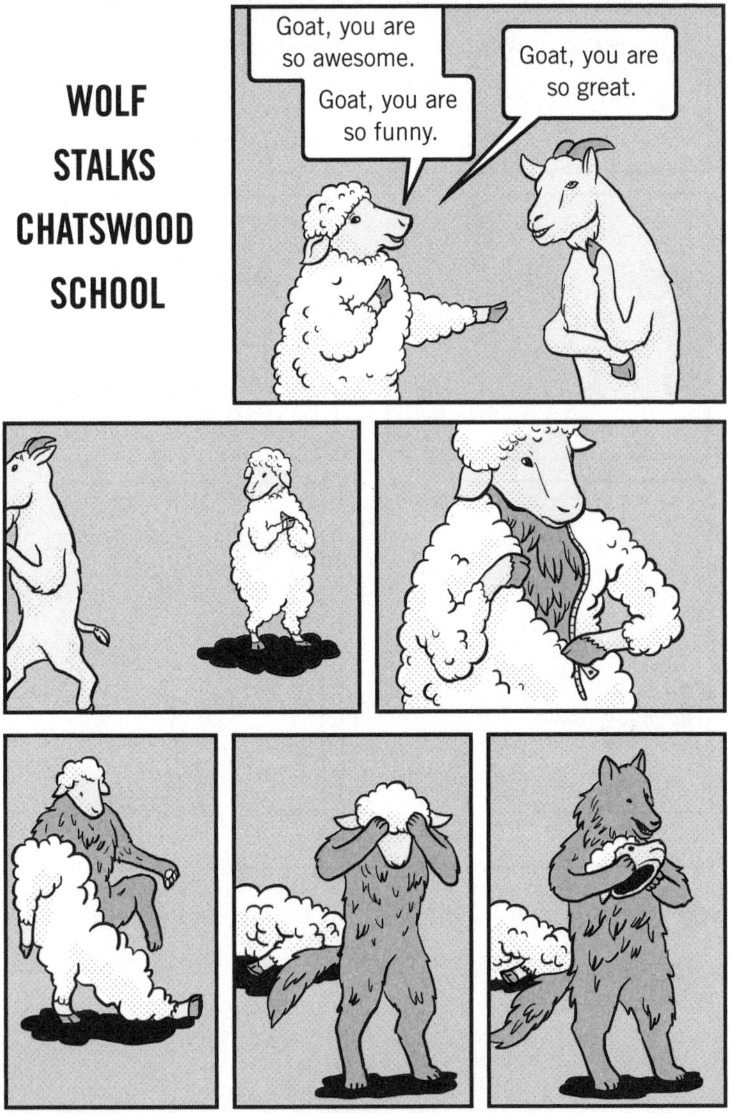

Goat, you are so awesome.
Goat, you are so funny.
Goat, you are so great.

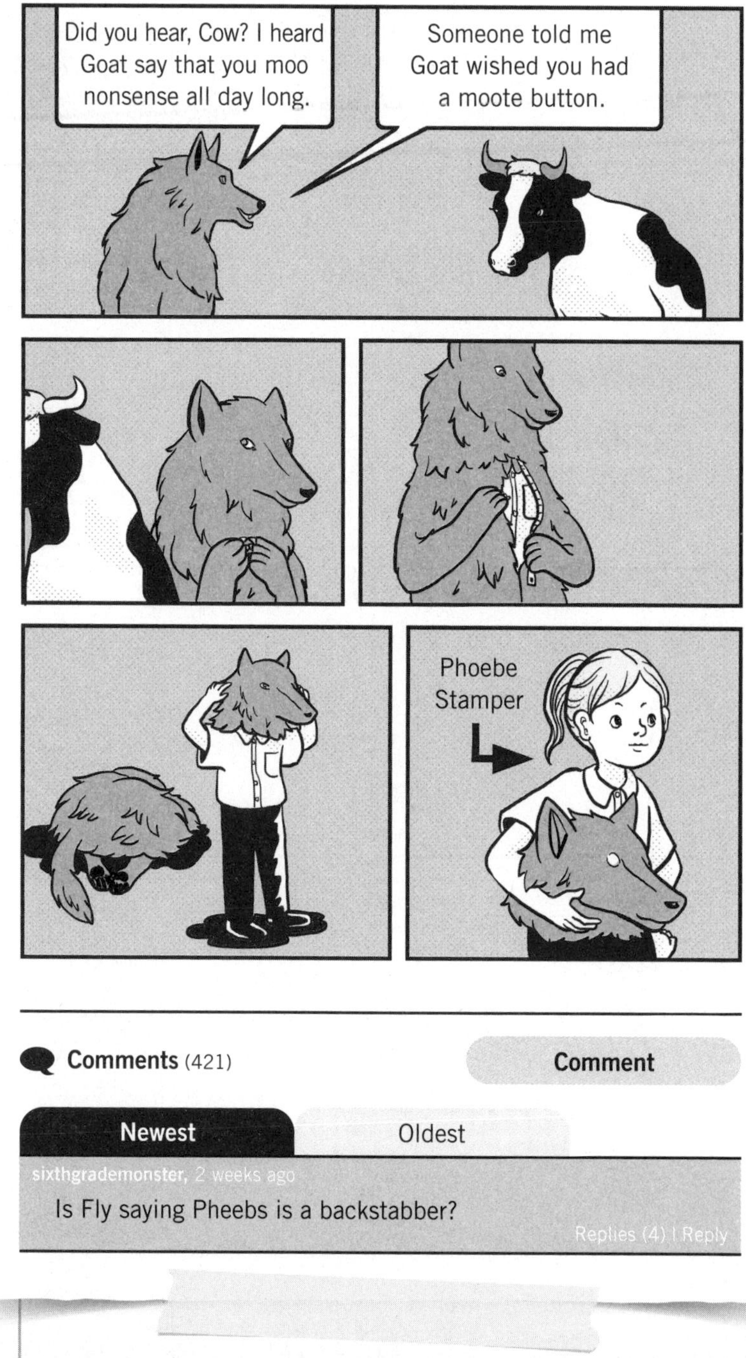
Did you hear, Cow? I heard Goat say that you moo nonsense all day long.
Someone told me Goat wished you had a moote button.
Phoebe Stamper

**Comments** (421)

**Comment**

**Newest** Oldest

sixthgrademonster, 2 weeks ago

Is Fly saying Pheebs is a backstabber?

Replies (4) | Reply

**tommy,** 4 weeks ago

But she seems so nice! We need deets, Fly!

Reply

**schoolstinks423,** 4 weeks ago

She's not like that at all. Fly on the Wall is a jerk.

Replies (1) | Reply

**donutandcake,** 4 weeks ago

I'd better keep away from her.

Replies (12) | Reply

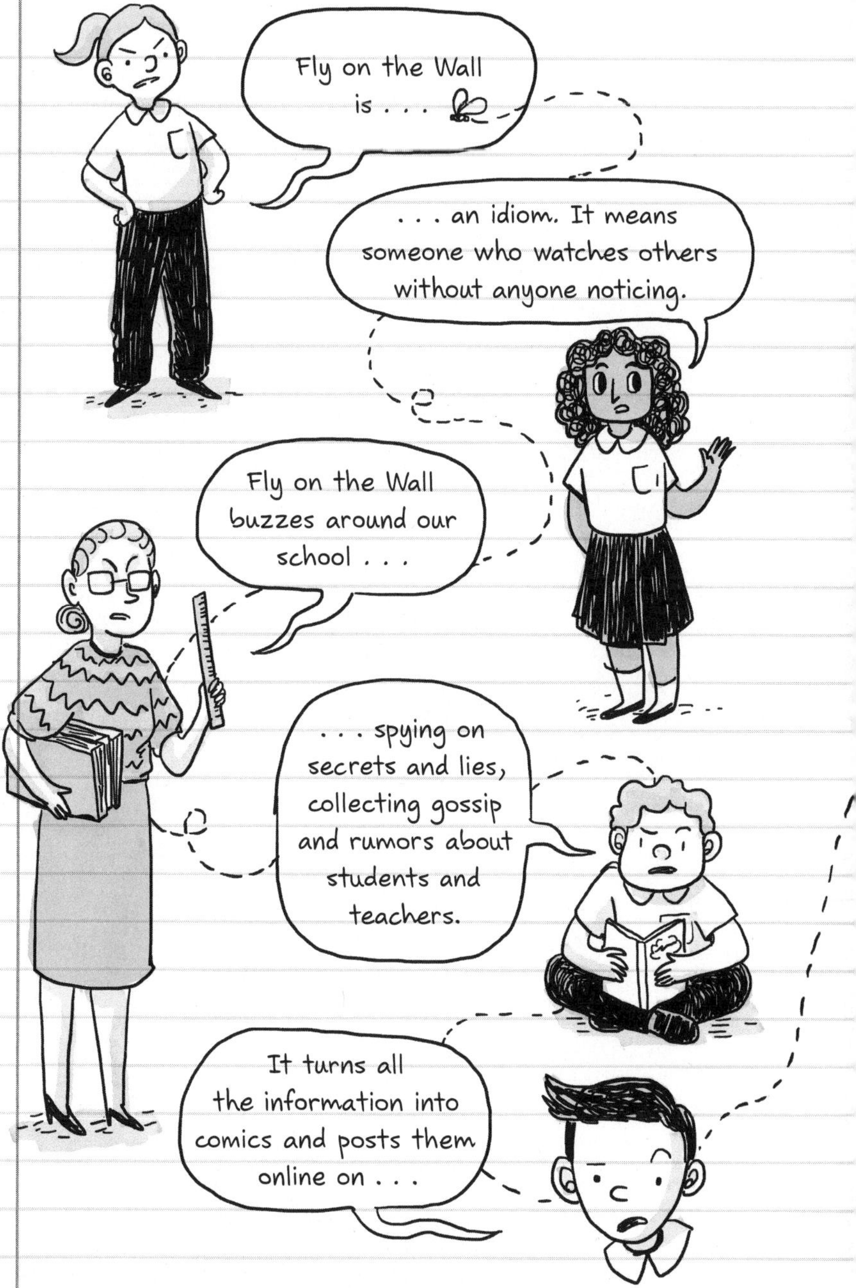

Fly on the Wall is . . .
. . . an idiom. It means someone who watches others without anyone noticing.
Fly on the Wall buzzes around our school . . .
. . . spying on secrets and lies, collecting gossip and rumors about students and teachers.
It turns all the information into comics and posts them online on . . .

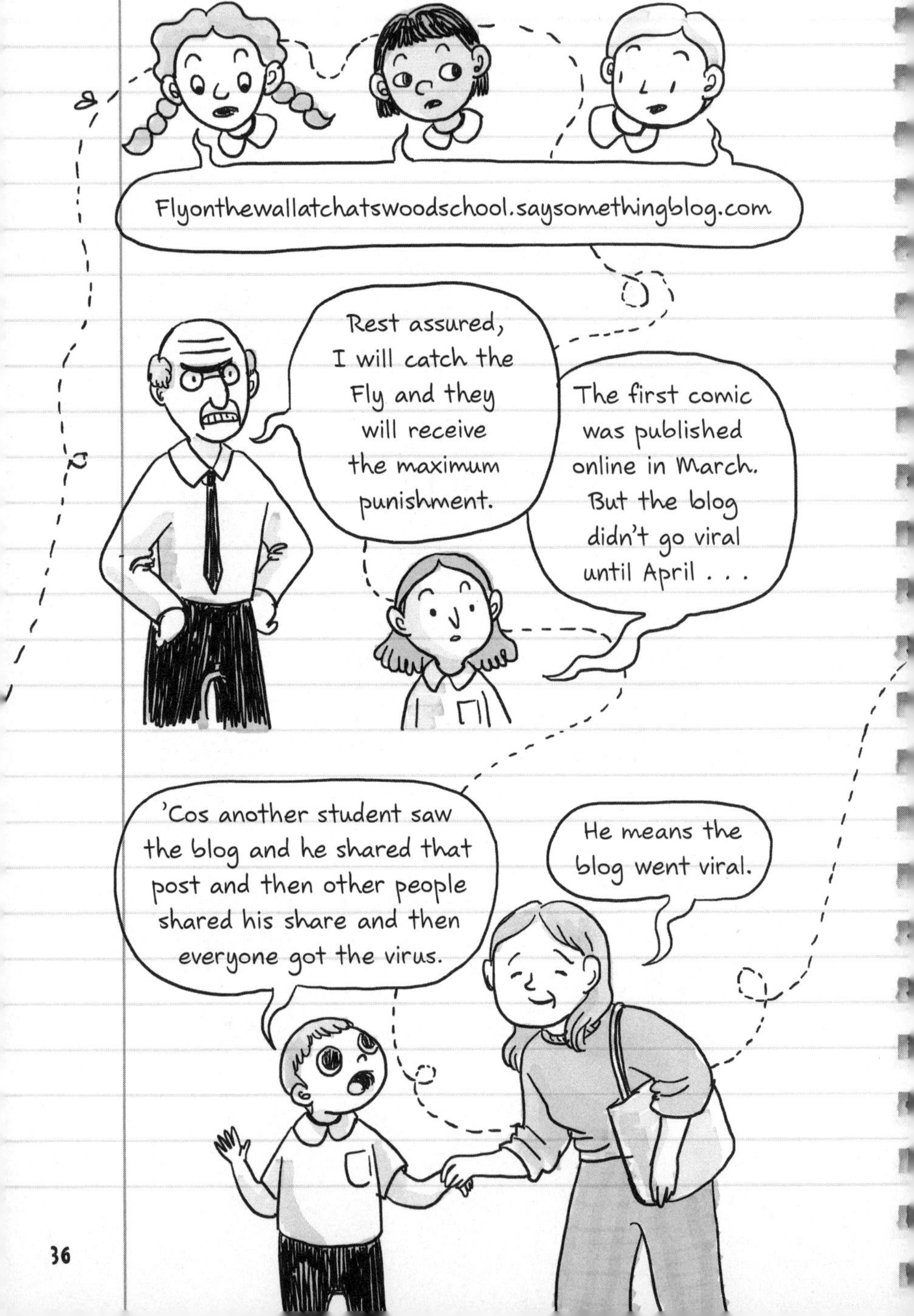
Flyonthewallatchatswoodschool.saysomethingblog.com
Rest assured, I will catch the Fly and they will receive the maximum punishment.
The first comic was published online in March. But the blog didn't go viral until April . . .
'Cos another student saw the blog and he shared that post and then other people shared his share and then everyone got the virus.
He means the blog went viral.

It was me! I made the blog go viral! In April, I was searching "Chatswood School" when I discovered the *Fly on the Wall* blog.

Of course I've heard about Fly on the Wall.

苍蝇在哪儿? 不是在桌子上的那碗药膳鸡汤吧? (Where's the fly? It's not on the bowl of herbal chicken soup on the table, is it?)

Fly on the Wall should be . . .

SPLAT!

**COUNTDOWN TO FLIGHT**

`0` `2` `3` `7`

**HOURS     MINUTES**

Still standing at Pheebs's front yard

Jie continues her interrogation. "How are your grades lately, Pheebs? Have they improved?"

Pheebs raises one eyebrow. She doesn't know the lie I fed my family to explain why she and I haven't been hanging out. "What's wrong with my—

AAA!

HI-YA!

HI-YA!

Uh . . . An ant climbed up my leg. I thought it was a poisonous spider.

HI-YA!

You're so dramatic.

RIIIING!

Excuse me.

Pheebs smiles at me as I pass her Maomi's leash.
The number of knives she's secretly sharpening could
be one or a hundred.

But it could also be zero. That smile looks the
same as all her other smiles.

Maybe time has healed some wounds. Maybe her
wearing that *HI-YA!* T-shirt is her smoke signal that
we're okay. After Jie leaves, I'll tell Pheebs all about
the greatest adventure everrr.

"That was Popo," Jie says, hanging up. "I have
to drive her to the grocery store. Pheebs, one last
question: Tim Aditya is not in this project group, is he?"

Pheebs glances at me, then shakes her head. She must have heard, too, about how Tim Aditya gave me a black eye last month.

"Good." Jie climbs into our family's tortoise-green Toyota, rolls down the window, and waves at us as she pulls out of Pheebs's driveway. "Have fun, Henry! Make more friends! Pick you up at five!"

Bye, Jie!

Pheebs, there's something I want to tell you—

Pheebs's smile has been towed away by the Toyota.

I'll look after Maomi until five o'clock.

click

Pheebs doesn't ask, doesn't care, where I'll be for the next nine hours. For all she knows, I could be hanging out with the *bad crowd* at wherever it is they hang out and ruining my whole future.

She appears at her large window. Maomi rests his chin on the windowsill. Behind them, on the wall, are Pheebs's and my yellow handprints. She's the right hand, and I'm the left. We painted them on that wall when we were little. Her dads were horrified when they saw our "artwork." I cried, thinking we were going to be punished, but they decided the paintings were cute and left the masterpieces there.

Her eyes cast down at the space next to my feet, where there's a swirl of—might be Maomi's—turd. That's the same way she's been looking at me for the past six months, like I'm . . .

I get that feeling again. A cup about to overflow. A balloon about to Pop! A volcano about to BOOM! To distract myself, I quickly cross the yard to the edge of the street and wait for a taxi.

BEEP!

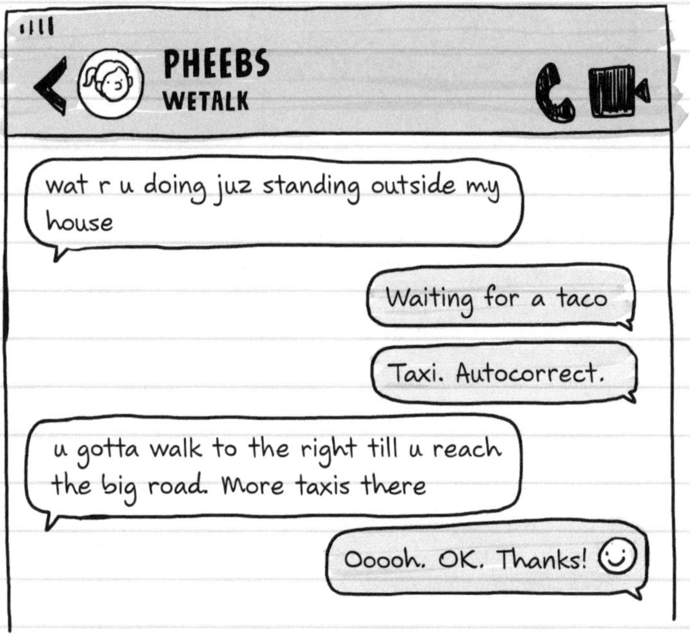
PHEEBS
WETALK
wat r u doing juz standing outside my house
Waiting for a taco
Taxi. Autocorrect.
u gotta walk to the right till u reach the big road. More taxis there
Ooooh. OK. Thanks!

After that, Pheebs doesn't reply. Not even a smiley face.

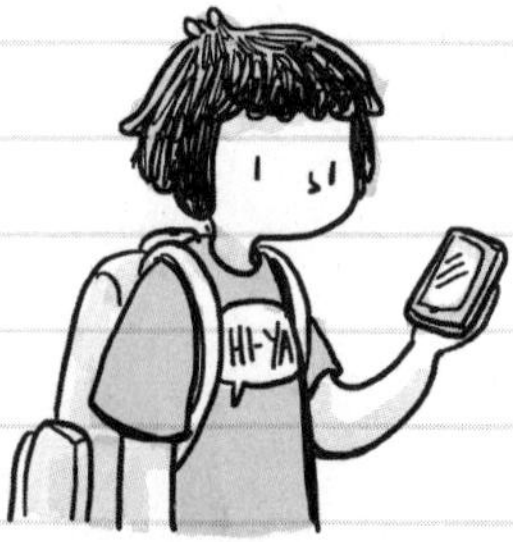
HI-YA

Suddenly, it hits me:

From here on, I'm truly on my own.

I've never gone anywhere by myself. Except when I walk Maomi along the tracks in the forest at the end of my street. Although that doesn't really count, since Maomi is with me and Popo waits for me at the picnic area at the start of the tracks.

She's supposed to supervise me, but she said her knees collect water inside. That makes it painful for her to walk far. Her watery knees are also why she stopped walking me home from school this year, and Mom took over. "I'd come along on walks," Popo said, "if I could ride a horse like my wuxia heroes."

I've been so excited about going on the adventure I didn't think to be nervous. It's like when you eat something super spicy, and your tongue's so on fire that all you can think about is the chili pepper, not about the salt or sugar or other flavors.

But if I want my family to stop thinking I'm a baby . . .

If I want them to never annoy Pheebs again . . .

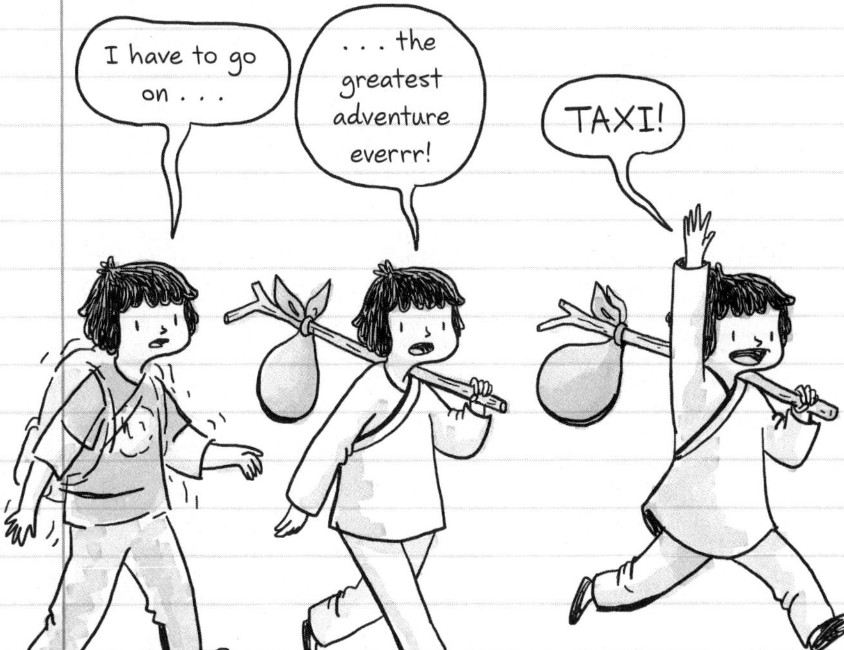
I have to go on . . .
. . . the greatest adventure everrr!
TAXI!

THERE ARE
NO TAXIS
AVAILABLE

TAXI

I wait
and wait.
RRRRING!
!
金隆，你不是需要你的虎爪吗？为什么把它留在你的抽屉里？
(Henry, don't you need your tiger claw? Why did you leave it in your drawer?)

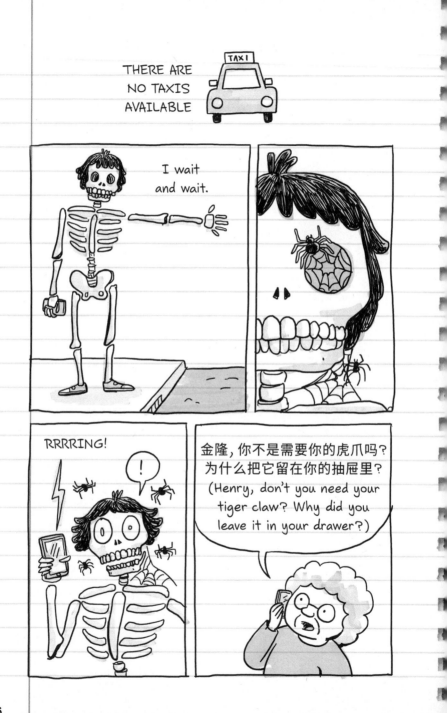

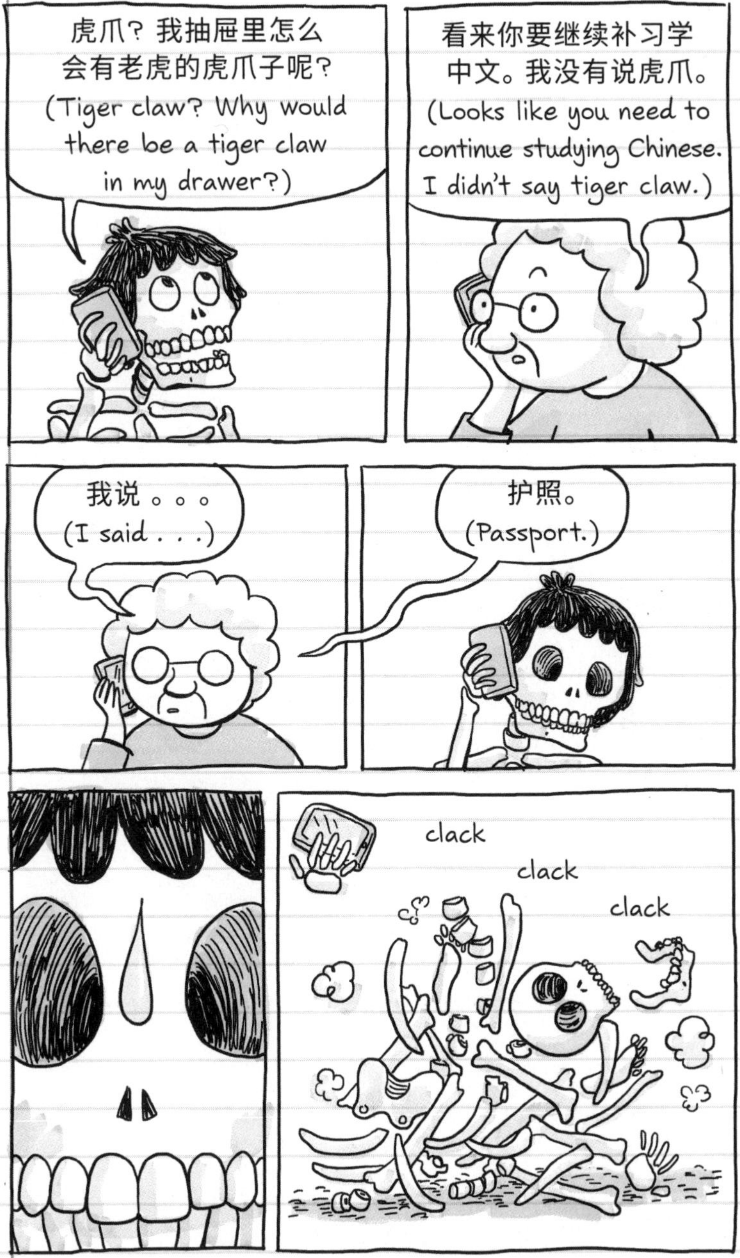

虎爪？我抽屉里怎么会有老虎的虎爪子呢？
(Tiger claw? Why would there be a tiger claw in my drawer?)
看来你要继续补习学中文。我没有说虎爪。
(Looks like you need to continue studying Chinese. I didn't say tiger claw.)
我说。。。
(I said . . .)
护照。
(Passport.)
clack
clack
clack

Without a passport, I won't be able to fly. The Plan is about to be crushed like bones in Maomi's jaws. That thought would have made regular Henry cry, but not Lone Wanderer Henry.

One time, Jie ate my last pudding cup and I cried and cried. I don't know why. Pudding cups aren't even my favorite snack. Popo said I was just really tired because I'd had a big day—I'd gone on a class trip to the botanical gardens, and the sun was beaming down all day, giving me a headache.

Tired? Nah.

Henry's just too emotional.

I want to be the right amount of emotional. On this adventure, I'm not going to cry even once. Forgetting my passport will not reduce me to tears. After all, in wuxia dramas, the lone wanderers and disciples face many obstacles. Popo often gets carried away like she's the shifu and shouts at the

TV, "吃一堑，长一智。" It means "a fall in a pit, a gain in wit." Getting over this obstacle, figuring out how to make the flight, will make me wiser.

Ten minutes later, I'm hiding behind a big bush in my front yard, trying to catch my breath. I rummage in my pockets to fish out my key . . . only to remember I don't have one! Not because I lost it, but because I never had one to begin with. I'm always with either Popo, Mom, or Jie—people who have keys and the privilege to lose them.

But I will not be so easily thwarted. To sneak into the house, I have to be nimble and stealthy, like a . . .

JAPANESE NINJA!

I find my passport in my drawer, exactly where Popo said it would be. This mission is as easy as pie.

As I'm sneaking away, I hear Jie talking. From somewhere else in the house, she says, "Hey, Dad."

*WHAT IS DAD DOING HERE?*

"Mom's at the farmers' market. Popo is watching wuxia. And Henry . . . Hold on for a sec, Dad, let me finish this text . . ."

Phew. It's just Jie on the phone with Dad. But that's strange. I can't recall the last time Dad called Jie or me outside of our weekly Saturday-night video calls.

BEEP!

That's my phone! My very LOUD phone.

"Wait, Dad. I heard something . . . in Henry's room. But he's at Pheebs's. Don't tell me that Bao Bao forgot his phone . . ."

Footsteps approach.

EEP!

## COUNTDOWN TO FLIGHT

| 0 | 2 | | 1 | 4 |
|---|---|---|---|---|
| **HOURS** | | | **MINUTES** | |

In my own bedroom, my death imminent

There's no time to scramble out the window.

Footsteps grow louder.

Louder.

Closer.

I ninja-roll on the floor and duck under my desk just as Jie trespasses into my room.

"Hmm, no one's here." She sits on the chair. If she kicks her leg out, I'll be busted. Turns out, this mission is not as easy as pie, but as challenging as pi, the mathematical constant used in complicated math. "I must have heard a noise from outside . . ."

I quickly fish out my phone, turn it to silent, and reply to Jie's message.

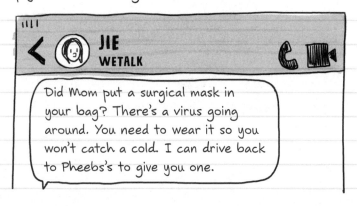

JIE
WETALK

Did Mom put a surgical mask in your bag? There's a virus going around. You need to wear it so you won't catch a cold. I can drive back to Pheebs's to give you one.

The ninja has great immunity, although he did once sneeze snot all over Jie. Families are overenthusiastic tattoo artists. You make a tiny mistake just one time, and it's like they immediately ink that thing onto you forever.

When people tell you enough times what you are, after a while you start to believe them.

"*Fly on the Wall*?" Jie says. "I check that ridiculous blog every week, Dad. There's no mention of Henry."

I can't make out Dad's words on the other end, but he sounds very far away. When we video call him every Saturday night on the computer in the living room, his face fills the screen and his voice is loud and clear, as if he's right here in Perth with us. Now his voice is mumbled as if he's telling Jie secrets.

Secrets I'm kept out of.

Dad also sounds weird because of the multiple long sentences he's saying to Jie. When he and I talk, it's usually all short questions like *Have you eaten?* and *When are your exams?* and short answers like *Yes* and *Today*. He probably thinks I'm a baby who can't understand multiple long sentences, and I don't blame him, thanks to two hovering helicopters.

HOVERRRHOVERRRR

JIE

MOM

You've turned me into a helipad!

I'm sure Dad loves me. He never hits or scolds me, and he buys me all the books I want and most of the toys I want. But does he like me?

Not very much.

I can tell because we don't do anything that dads and sons on TV do, like kick a ball around or go fishing or spend some quality time camping in the woods, just the two of us, with the bugs and the snakes.

But that's not how I know for sure he doesn't like me. The evidence came after I ran into a door at school and hurt my eye. Mom took me to the doctor's, and when the doctor was gazing into my eye, Mom's phone rang. She stepped into the hall outside to answer Dad's video call. She left the door ajar, and I caught bits and pieces of their conversation.

"Were you in a meeting when I called earlier?" Mom said. "Yes . . . It's Henry . . . The doctor's examining him now . . . A kid hit him . . . Not sure . . . his left eye . . . Looks bad . . ."

"How could . . . I see . . . ," Dad said. "*Sigh* . . . I wish . . . ."

I wish Henry hadn't been born.

Don't hate my dad. He isn't a bad guy. He just prefers his kids to not be so helpless, just like I prefer my toast crusty. But I can change Dad's opinion of me. Once I'm in Singapore, without those helicopters, I'll have many opportunities to show him that I can do things on my own.

Maybe then, he won't just love me, but also like me.

Jie crosses her legs so that one foot is right in front of my eyeball. If those sharp painted toenails come any closer, I'll get pink eye. And the first aid kit in my bag doesn't have a cure for that.

"Yeah, I did ask Henry," she says. "He has no idea who Fly could be."

Why is Dad asking about Fly? How does Dad even know about Fly?

From somewhere else in the house, Popo shouts, "苍蝇在哪里？最好不是在桌子上的那盘梅菜扣肉。" (Where's the fly? It'd better not be on that plate of preserved pork and vegetables on the table!)

Jie shouts back, "I've told you this before, Popo, it's not a real fly!"

Popo doesn't reply. She often ignores English Jie.

"Dad, has Mom told you?" Jie says. "Principal Trang called two special assemblies last month. He talked to the students about Fly and even tried to get them to rat Fly out. No one did, of course. I don't think anyone knows who Fly is. But it's not a surprise that Principal Trang is desperate to trap the Fly. I mean, issue number two? That's brutal."

# FLY ON THE WALL

**CHATSWOOD SCHOOL PRINCIPAL CAUSES THE PLAGUE**

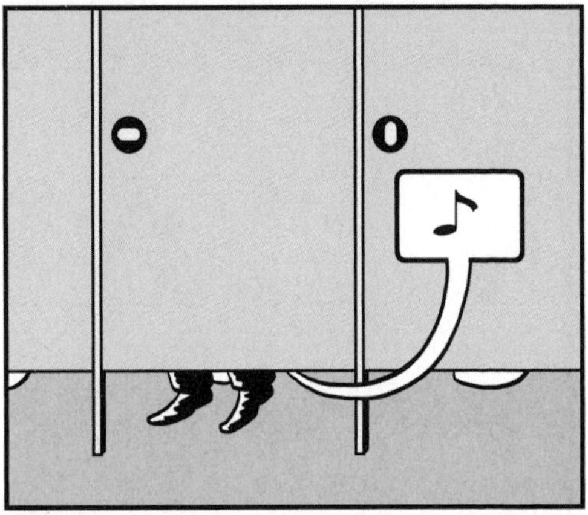

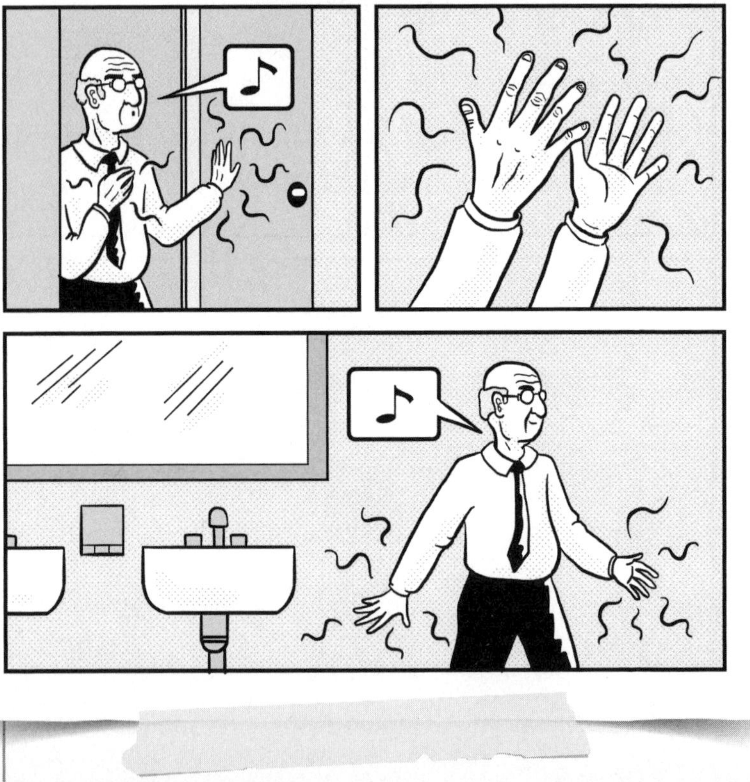

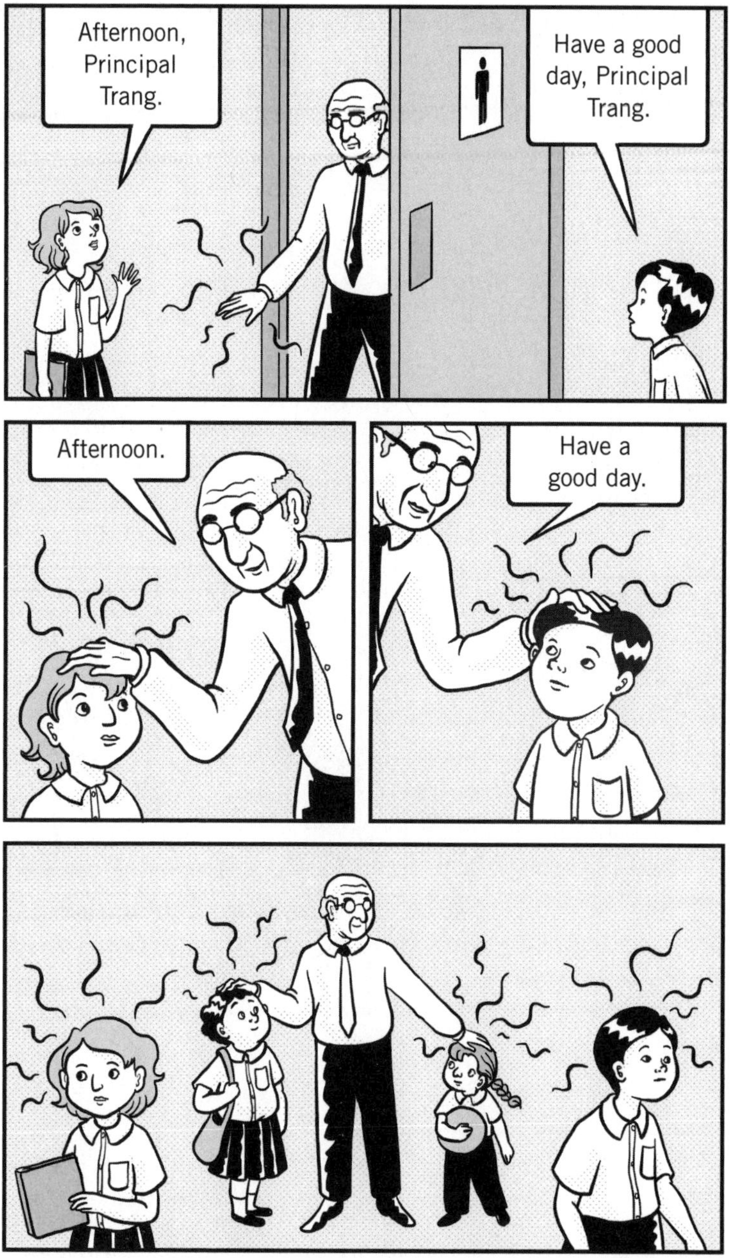
Afternoon, Principal Trang.
Have a good day, Principal Trang.
Afternoon.
Have a good day.

*Not* in a cab heading for the airport

Jie swings her foot. Thanks to my ninja reflex, I duck in time.

"Dad, I've never seen Principal Trang that furious. He said, 'Rest assured, everyone. I will personally hunt down the Fly, and when I catch the culprit, I'm going to squash them like a bug.'"

I gulp. Silently. Then I shudder.

The truth is, for the past few months, I've been hiding a deep, dark secret.

A secret that, if revealed, will put me in the deep and dark of a coffin six feet underground.

I, Henry Khoo . . .

am Fly on the Wall.

Dad, have you read this email Mom just forwarded us? The one from Principal Trang?

I open my email.

---

⊡ ⊞ ✉ ···

↩ ···

**FWD: SUBJECT:** Fly on the Wall
[inbox]

**FROM:** khoofamily@geemail.com
**TO:** henrykhoo@geemail.com, hayleykhoo@geemail.com, robertkhoo@geemail.com

Dear family,

I WAS worried that Fly on the Wall might one day post something nasty about Henry. But this email is good news!

I'll be back home soon. The farmers' market is packed!

-Mom

>>>>>> Begin Forwarded Message >>>>>>
**FROM:** principal@chatswoodschool.edu.au
**TO:** khoofamily@geemail.com
**SUBJECT:** Fly on the Wall

---

Dear parents and guardians,

I'm writing to allay your fears. Rest assured that the school is doing its best to investigate the matter of the anonymous blogger Fly on the Wall. We are confident this will be resolved soon. Rest assured that the student involved will be appropriately dealt with.

Best,
Principal Trang

P.S. Rest assured that contrary to Fly on the Wall's comic, our cafeteria does NOT and will NEVER serve roadkill meat pie.

↩ REPLY     ↪ FORWARD

What evidence could Principal Trang have dug up? Now that I think of it . . .

HI-YA!

There was that one time in the computer lab . . . I have to escape before Principal Trang catches me!

But I'm trapped here.

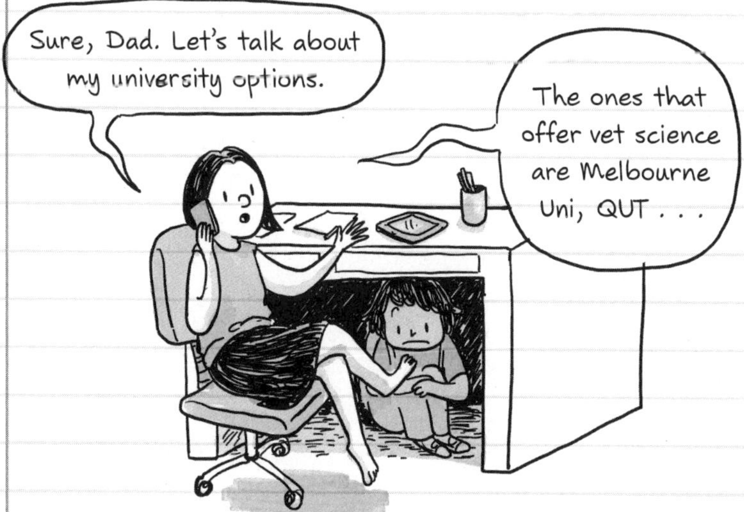
Sure, Dad. Let's talk about my university options.
The ones that offer vet science are Melbourne Uni, QUT . . .

Luckily, at that moment, Popo's F grade in technology saves me.

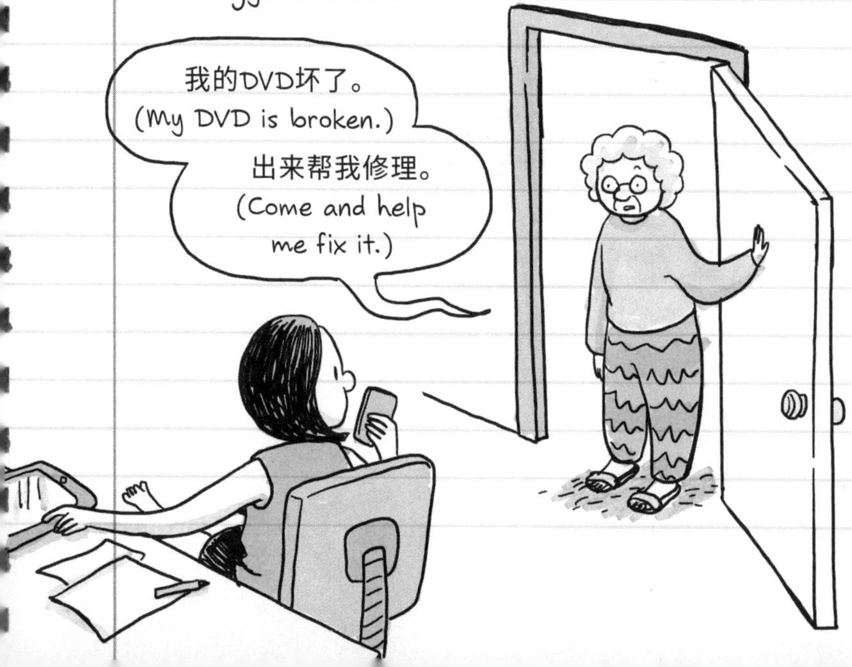
我的DVD坏了。
(My DVD is broken.)
出来帮我修理。
(Come and help me fix it.)

Popo adds, "那个主角快要拜师学武术和人生道理。" (The main character is about to become a disciple to learn martial arts and life wisdom.)

"Dad, I have to help Popo again," Jie says, getting up. "Could you call me back in ten minutes?"

Once the coast is clear, I transform back into the ninja and . . .

Rest assured, when Fly on the Wall's identity is exposed, I'll be far, far away from here.

## COUNTDOWN TO FLIGHT

**0 2 0 0**

**HOURS    MINUTES**

On the way to the airport. Finally!
In a taxi with permit number EY35XXXONXXXU

Help! My taxi driver, Neil, might be an undercover
FBI agent. He's asking me way too many questions.
My life is not that interesting.

Are you flying alone?

I'm very independent.

Why are you heading
to Singapore?

To visit my dad.

NEIL

Is your Dad
Singaporean?

Yes.

And your
mom?

Australian.

LIAR

lie
detector

To convince Neil that I'm old enough and therefore wise enough to travel on my own, I make my voice as deep as I can. I've had lots of practice, since I overheard Jie telling Mom that maybe I don't speak much because my voice is breaking. That means one moment I'm a chipmunk and the next moment I'm a mafia boss.

But Neil must be using some FBI interrogator technique to make me unknowingly confess that I'm an illegal underage adventurer. He's got skills, because somehow I end up telling him all the things that aren't his business, like how my parents didn't break up; they just live on different continents. They met in Perth, and after they got married, they moved to Singapore, which was where Jie and I were born. But Mom missed Australia. She brought Jie and me back to Popo's house here in Perth while Dad remained in Singapore to run his business and earn money to pay for our stuff.

"I love the food in Singapore," Neil says. "The Hainan chicken rice, the nasi lemak, the prata."

Neil is truly an A+ interrogator. He's using yummy food to distract me from being suspicious of him being suspicious of me.

I look out the window to make sure he's not driving us to the police station.

Waitaminute! I recognize the Sunshine Supermarket we're driving past. At the end of this road is a police station. Neil's going to turn me in!

Turns out, the building at the end of the road is not a police station but a . . .

Oops. I panicked for nothing.

But before I could sigh with relief, we drove past Origins Park—the park that sits between Pheebs's house and mine, the park where she had her birthday party last December. As memories of that day come flooding back, my heart beats fast as if I were running from a ghost.

Popo, Mom, and Jie acted like I'd been invited to the Queen's Fancy-Pants Tea Party. They all came along to drop me off at the park. Pheebs had invited all of our classmates, and seventeen showed up. The picnic tables were covered with boxes and boxes of pizza.

"Want to hear a joke about pizza?" Pheebs's dad said. "Never mind, it's too cheesy."

Pheebs rolled her eyes. "You promised no dad jokes today, Dad!"

"Oooooh," Austin Turner said. "These pizzas look like bicycle wheels."

A bicycle with pizza wheels would be nice. When you got tired and hungry from cycling, you could have a meal. The only problem is you couldn't cycle anymore after that.

"All right, all right," Pheebs's dad said. "Everyone, buddy up in twos."

I made a beeline toward Pheebs, since we were always partners in everything. But when I walked up to Pheebs, she had already lined her bicycle up next to Dee's.

"Sorry, Henry," Pheebs said. "Before I knew you were coming, I already promised Dee that I'd be her buddy."

Pheebs's pa walked up next to me. "Sorry, Henry, but you're matched up with this old dude," he said, smiling and pointing to himself.

"It's okay, I don't mind," I said. "I wasn't supposed to be here anyway." And that was the truth. I really didn't mind. If Pheebs knew I was coming, she'd have chosen me.

Or so I thought, until . . .

Yeah, Pa, Henry doesn't mind.

He's really not supposed to be here.

My head felt like it does whenever I slurp a Slurpee too fast—a mixture of numbness and pressure as if my brain's being squeezed. I couldn't do or say anything, since I had no idea what the feeling was and also zero idea why Pheebs's words made me feel that way. She was only stating a fact.

Pheebs pedaled away. In no time, I forgot about the brain-freeze feeling because I was preoccupied with making turns and braking and keeping up with everyone. I ended up having a fun time cycling around the park.

Toward the end of the party, everyone sat down at the benches, put on party hats, and scarfed down pizzas. That was new. I'd been around other kids besides Pheebs plenty of times in school, but we had a hi-bye kind of relationship. I'd hardly ever noticed them. I had Pheebs, and we had a let-me-tell-you-a-top-secret kind of relationship. It was perfect.

As the other kids talked and joked with one another, I watched them like a curious scientist observing rats in a maze. It was fascinating. But after a while, I suddenly became aware of something . . .

I didn't like being the scientist—on the outside, looking in.

HAHA!

Totally!

There was a must-know joke, and all the rats got it. I didn't. If someone had asked me then what I'd like to be when I grow up, I'd have answered a rat.

When all the pizzas were gone, I was relieved—until I found out we were all going to cycle back to Pheebs's house for dessert and more games. A little part of me wanted to teleport back to my room and just lie on the bed with Maomi, but another part wanted to stay and have fun with everyone. It didn't make sense, wanting to drop out yet not wanting to miss out. But in this world, not everything makes sense. Proof: Pizzas are made round when their boxes are square.

It was a short trip to Pheebs's house, along quiet streets, with Pheebs's dad and pa supervising us. Then, from behind us, we heard, "汪汪! (Woof woof!)"

Not too far behind us, driving along really, really slowly, was a green car. My family's Toyota.

汪汪!
(Woof woof!)

Dee said, "Henry, isn't that your family? What are they doing?"

Yangmei snorted with laughter. "Are they going to follow us all the way to Pheebs's house?"

Austin simply said, "Wow."

Pheebs said nothing. She just turned her head away, like she was trying to avoid my gaze.

Another car came up behind my family's Toyota. It was stuck behind our Tortoise Toyota. Then more cars got stuck.

汪汪!
(Woof woof!)

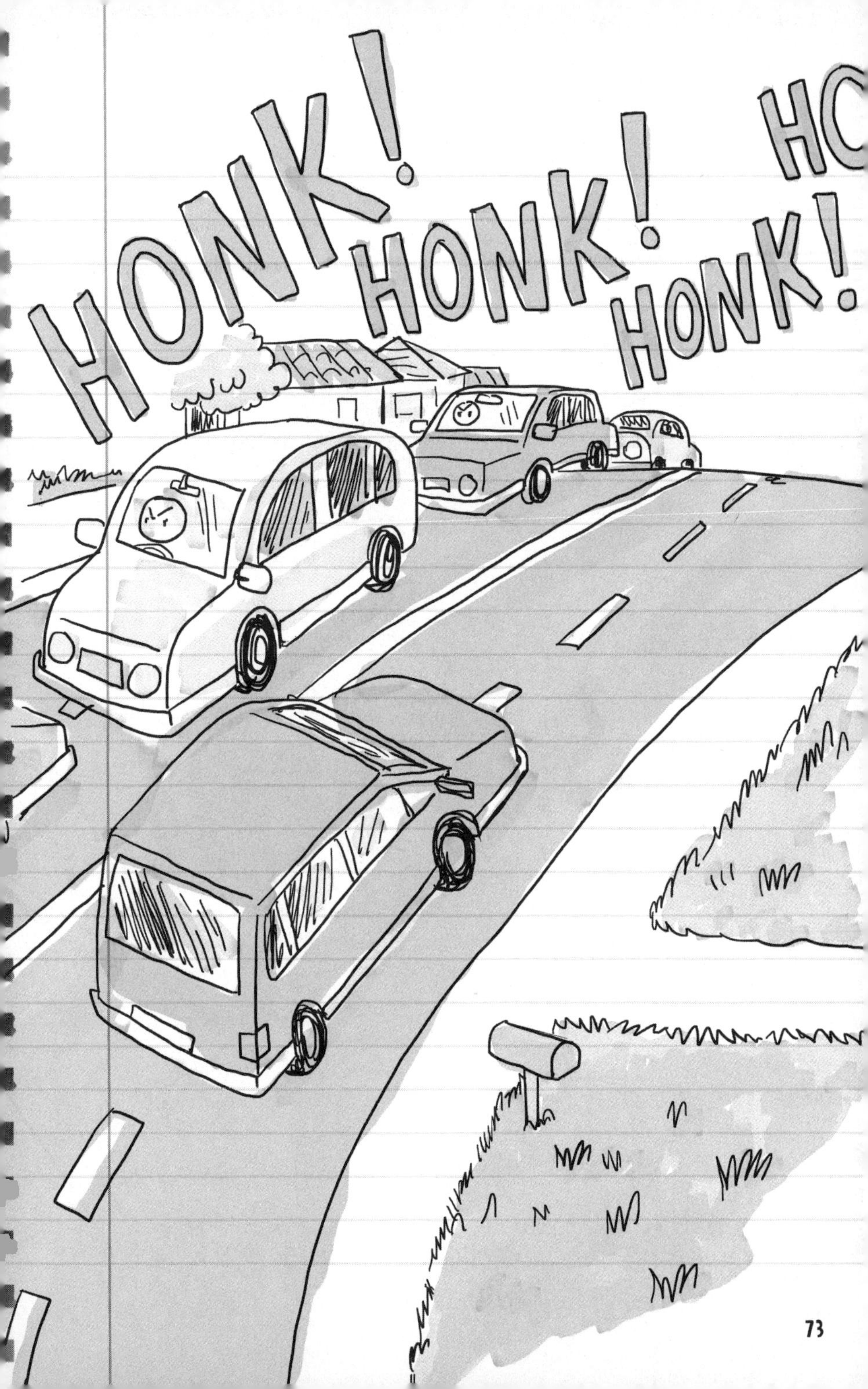
HONK!
HONK!
HONK!

Pheebs had this look on her face. She didn't look angry or sad. It was expressionless. I had never seen that on her.

I didn't know what it meant, but I got that brain-freeze feeling again.

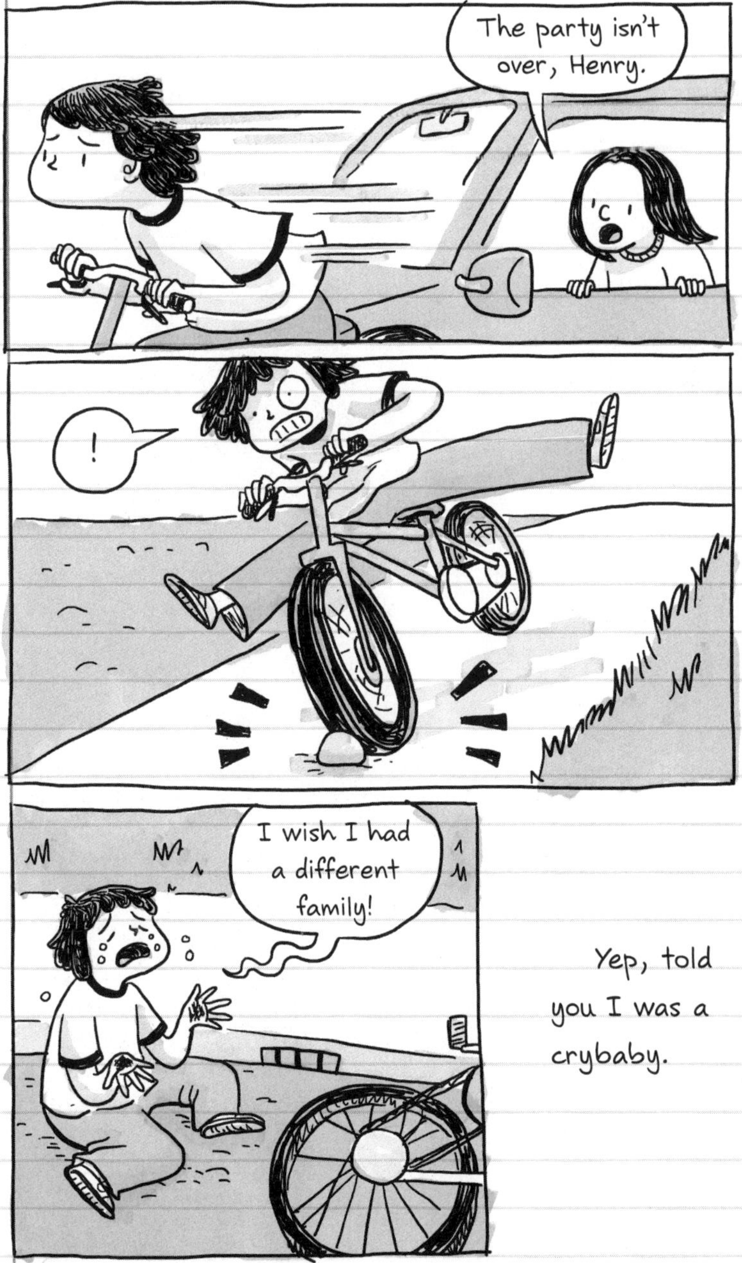
The party isn't over, Henry.
!
I wish I had a different family!

Yep, told you I was a crybaby.

I got a few deep cuts on my palms, and they burned when Mom cleaned and creamed and bandaged them. But turned out, the worst kind of hurt is invisible to the eye.

That night, as I lay in bed, my hands looking like the mummy of King Tutankhamen, I thought about what had happened. I do that a lot—think about the day's happenings, what someone said or did, what I said or what I did, long after they occurred. It's not that I purposely think about these things; they just float into my mind. Maybe my skull is too thick and it takes time for things to slowly seep through and reach my brain.

That night, long after the party was over, Pheebs's *he's really not supposed to be here* and her expressionless look reached my brain. They linked up to her surprised-but-maybe-not-in-a-good-way reaction when she had run into me outside my house the day before, which I also hadn't really thought about. There was something unsaid in those words and in those expressions. It was as if she was rolling her eyes without actually rolling them.

As if she wished I hadn't come to the party.

Suddenly, the taxi swerves. My seat belt digs into my chest. Is Neil trying to pump a confession out of me?

"Sorry," Neil says. "Almost took the wrong lane.

Would have ended up a long way away. You know, life is like a highway filled with multiple lanes and multiple exits. Take a different exit, travel in a different lane, and your life changes forever."

That's probably some kind of wise proverb. Neil is clearly trying to use complicated logic to confuse me into confessing.

But he is right.

If I hadn't gone to that party, Pheebs's *he's really not supposed to be here* wouldn't have happened. That's my fault. But Jie and Mom and Popo are 1,000 percent to blame for everything else. If they hadn't humiliated me and Pheebs by tailgating us in the Tortoise Toyota, Pheebs's blank expression and us becoming NRFFs wouldn't have happened. I wouldn't have started the gossip and rumor blog. That bicycle accident was the first step of Henry Khoo's Transformation into Fly on the Wall.

It's too late. I've gone too far down the road. My life has changed forever. There's nothing to do now but make sure I reach my destination— Singapore. There, I'll declare my independence.

There are two things I can do now to make sure The Plan is a success.

The first is resist Neil's sly interrogation.

The second is something that Mom thinks is a bigger crime than paying for parking. Mom is from Generation X. X for X-tra stingy. She'd rather circle around for five hours searching for a free spot than pay for parking. And at the supermarket, she always buys The Odd Bunch instead of the fresher stuff.

bags of misshapen veggies and fruits that are sold cheaply

"Neil," I say. "Take the highway! I'll pay the toll!"

**COUNTDOWN TO FLIGHT**

| 0 | 1 | | 4 | 5 |
|---|---|---|---|---|

**HOURS**    **MINUTES**

Toll fee: $10

Reaching the airport in 15 minutes: priceless

The departure hall is actually pretty cool and interesting. Without my family obstructing my view with their helicopter blades, the view is much better.

DEPARTURES

| FLIGHT | TIME | STATUS |
|--------|------|--------|
| SQ 223 | 09:30 | BOARDING |
| GA 776 | 09:40 | BOARDING |
| QF 125 | 09:55 | BOARDING |
| GA 213 | 09:55 | BOARDING |

giant screen that shows all the departing flights

luggage trolley—
to release the brakes,
press the handle

boy with a
backpack with
a leash

The little kid on the leash reminds me of Maomi.

BAHAHA! My family treats me like a pet!

HAHAHA

How's that funny?

. . .

. . .

"Everyone's funny bone is a different shape," I finally say to the nosy girl. Pheebs said I have a toilet-shaped funny bone because I love fart jokes. Pheebs's dad has a dad-shaped funny bone because he always makes dad jokes.

I don't really understand what "dad jokes" are. My dad never jokes with me.

"That's a myth," the girl says. "A funny bone isn't really a bone." She turns to a man and woman standing behind her. "Right, Mom? Dad?"

"I think it's a nerve . . . ," her dad says.

She taps on her phone. "Yep, Google says it's a nerve in your arm. That's why it feels funny when you bump it."

Different-shaped funny bones aren't a myth. I have evidence. Take the comments on Fly on the Wall's blog post for issue number five.

# FLY ON THE WALL

## A MOUSE IN CHATSWOOD SCHOOL CAFETERIA!

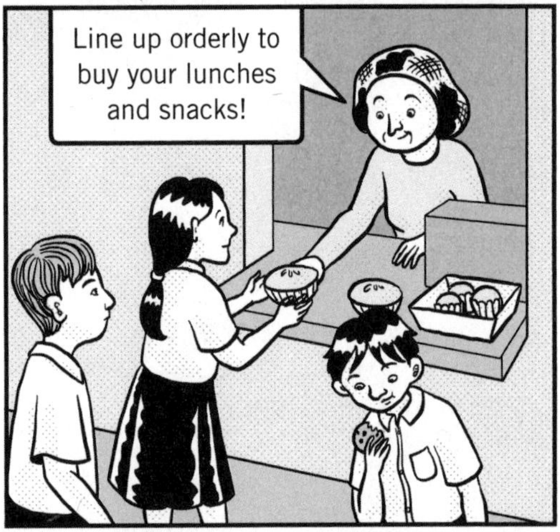
Line up orderly to buy your lunches and snacks!

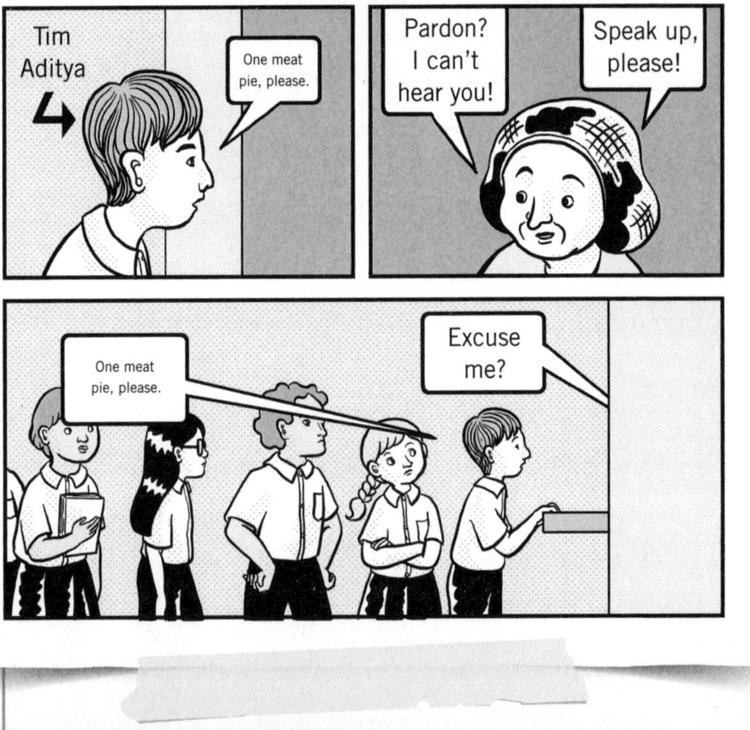
Tim Aditya
One meat pie, please.
Pardon? I can't hear you!
Speak up, please!
One meat pie, please.
Excuse me?

Some commenters clearly love the Fly, while others think he needs to perfume his bottom.

The funny-bone girl's dad kneels down so that he's actually eye to eye with her. "How are you feeling about the flight?"

She throws her arm around him. "I'm so excited!"

The girl and her dad remind me of the fathers and daughters in regular TV dramas, which I watch during the rare times Popo isn't hogging the TV for her wuxia dramas.

TV Kids often get into trouble, but at the end of the day, TV Parents always sit them down for heart-to-heart talks. TV Families are a little like Pheebs's family. Her pa is always asking her, *How was your day? Want to talk about it? You know I love you, right?*

When I ask Mom things like *Why do you like*

*Dad? Do you miss Dad? Does Dad miss us?* Mom replies, *Have you eaten? Are you hungry? How about a cookie or some noodles?*

And it's not just feelings stuff that my family doesn't talk about. When I ask Jie, *Why does Mom love cooking so much? Why must you drag me along when you go out with your friends when Popo's home to watch me? Why has Mom been walking me home from school recently instead of Popo?* Jie replies, *You'll understand when you're older.*

The only actual answers I get are to questions like *What's for lunch? Can we drop by the bookstore? Should we buy a horse for Popo?* (Fried rice. Yes. Not in a million years.)

It's like my family and I are all TV actors, but I don't have the script, so I'm just fumbling along. All my lines are wrong. That's why everyone else doesn't know how to act alongside me. Proof: Jie and Dad speak with each other in multiple long sentences. Dad and I do not.

By the time I complete my adventure and get to Dad's apartment, I will be a totally different Henry. I'll have the script and have even memorized it. I'll be so good I'll win an Emmy Award for Best Actor in the role of Perfect, Likable Son. Standing onstage for my thank-you speech, I'll give a shout-out to my shifu, the one I'll meet on this adventure, for teaching me the Art of Conversation.

"You want to hear a joke that is actually funny?" the girl asks me, as if I'm her BFF and not a stranger she just met a minute ago. "It's about pizza."

"But you can't tell me because it's too cheesy?"

"No, but that is funny!" She throws her head back and laughs. "What pizza does a dog like?"

"Umm . . . all kinds?"

"No! PUPperoni."

HAHAHA!

That's a good one!

girl's dad

I'm too big to be scooped up like that, but maybe my dad did that with me when I was little.

If he did, I wish I remembered.

"I gotta go check in," I say, and walk away. But I've only taken two steps when . . .

!

HI-YA!

Right in front of me is a sight that makes my eyes sore. This person is the unscratchable itch, the chocolate chips in your cookie that turn out to be raisins, the sesame seed that gets stuck between your teeth, the stubborn cowlick your mom keeps trying to smooth down with her spit.

He is my enemy, the bane of my existence, garlic to a vampire.

Worst of all, he is the person who saw me publish a *Fly on the Wall* post in the computer lab. He is none other than . . .

TIM ADITYA

SNAP!

SNAP!

In Popo's wuxia dramas, usually the villain's motive is:

    A) absolute power,

    B) untold riches,

    C) ultimate revenge,

    D) all of the above.

The answer is always obvious, because the villain states it clearly while cackling evilly. But Tim Aditya, he makes me scratch my head like I need antidandruff shampoo. He stumbled upon me making a *Fly on the Wall* post in the computer lab a month ago, after the issue on the mouse was published. He should have been angry and tattled on me. Yet he never did.

There's no reason why he should rat me out after all this time, but him being here in the flesh makes me break out in a cold sweat.

## MY MOST SINCERE PRAYER EVER

Dear Popo's Deities,

It's Henry Khoo here.

Please do something about Tim Aditya,

a witness to my crime,

a reminder that the secrecy
of my identity as
Fly on the Wall
is in peril,
especially with
Principal Trang hunting.
If I never had to see Tim Aditya again,
rest assured that I'd complain less
when Popo drags me to the temple.
And I'd burn more joss sticks as an offering
in exchange for your protection.
Thank you, Deities!
Sincerely, Henry Khoo

As I'm about to take myself far, far away from
Tim, I overhear:

WHAT DOES THAT SMIRK MEAN?

A) I'm up to something.

B) You will be in a world of pain.

C) I'm just trying to make you think I'm up
    to something.

D) All of the above.

I wish all villains could be like the ones in wuxia
dramas. They wear dark clothing and live in dark
caves and have raspy voices and they also tell you
outright they want to kill you.

Tim, he's as mysterious as the filling in my school
cafeteria's meat pie.

# FLY ON THE WALL

## CHATSWOOD SCHOOL STUDENTS DINE ON KOALA

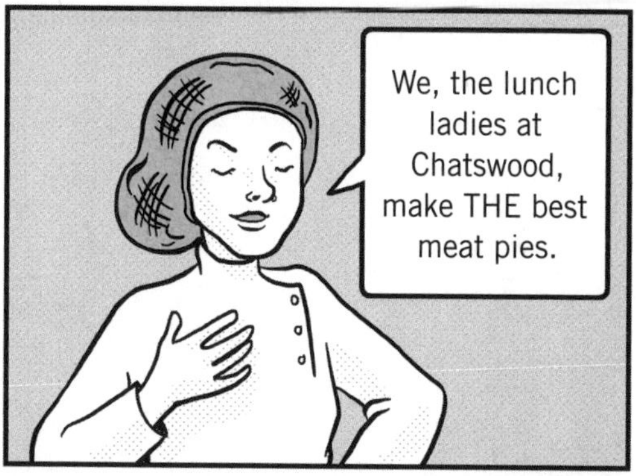
We, the lunch ladies at Chatswood, make THE best meat pies.

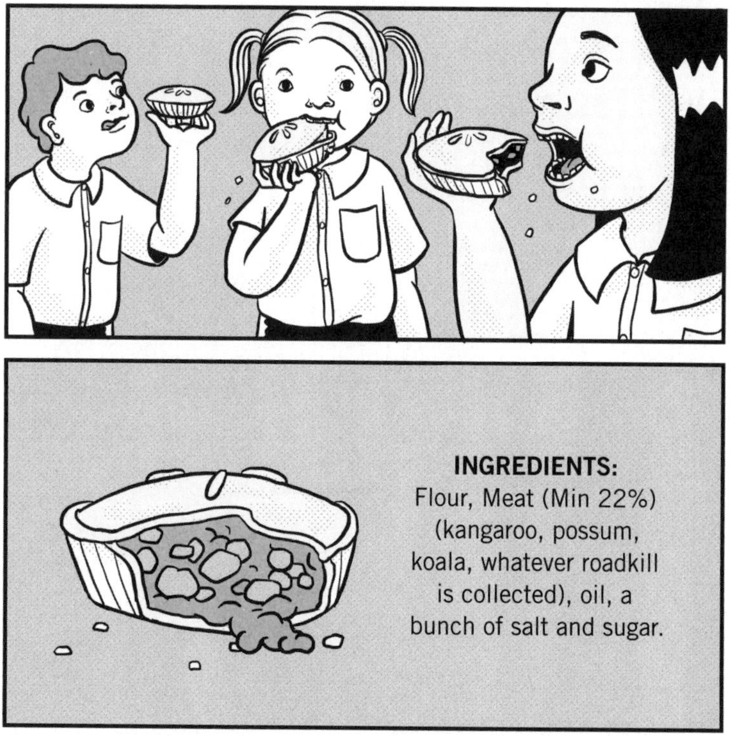
INGREDIENTS:
Flour, Meat (Min 22%) (kangaroo, possum, koala, whatever roadkill is collected), oil, a bunch of salt and sugar.

Tim walks away, traipsing behind his parents, and I wish I were him. His parents trust him so much and have total confidence in him. Not once do they turn back to check that he hasn't become lost or been kidnapped or gotten a stuffy nose.

That kind of freedom must be like swimming at the public pool when no one else is around. Tim can lazily float around or happily splash about. At my pool, it's always a summer day, there's always a heat wave, and it's always Aquarobics for Seniors time.

BZZ!

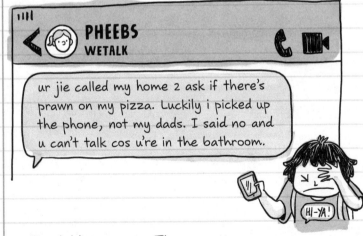

**PHEEBS**
WETALK

ur jie called my home 2 ask if there's prawn on my pizza. Luckily i picked up the phone, not my dads. I said no and u can't talk cos u're in the bathroom.

HI-YA!

I quickly message Jie.

92

> I was in the bathroom for normal bodily functions. No prawns on my pizza. I'm busy with my project. Don't call Pheebs again, OK? Why don't you watch wuxia with Popo?

I read Pheebs's message again. That's the most she has messaged me in a while. But maybe my phone won't be so silent once I gain independence. With The Plan in my mind, I hurry to the check-in area.

Checking in for a flight is like when your homeroom teacher takes attendance, except your teacher is a

**CHECK-IN KIOSK**

also prints boarding passes, which are like movie tickets that tell you which theater to go to and which seat to sit in

touch screen

I could have checked in online, but in the last forty-eight hours, there was not a minute when Mom or Jie wasn't in the busybody radius of the computer in the living room. If it were just Popo who was around, that'd be fine because she doesn't understand the internet. Besides, her eyes would be on the wuxia battle on the TV, not on the computer screen.

"Where are your parents?" a voice behind me asks. An airline staffer, with blue-green jacket and pants, towers over me.

If only I had a forest of facial hair to make me look older. "I'm twelve. It's not against the law for me to fly on my own."

Even though I'm right, even though I've researched the different airline policies and confirmed kids twelve and older can travel on their own on the airline I'm taking, even though I stand on tiptoes to make myself look my age, the woman furrows her eyebrows. She looks around. "Didn't your parents even come to send you off?"

I mentioned that I'm very average, but actually, sometimes, when it comes to the speed at which I think on my feet, I'm way slower.

"They don't seem to have noticed that they've left you behind," the airline staffer says. "Aren't you going to call out to them?"

"The . . . thing . . . is . . ." Nervous sweat pools in my underarms. "They're trying to give me opportunities to do things on my own." Luckily, before I drown the world in my sweat, the kiosk spits out my boarding pass.

| ECONOMY CLASS | ECONOMY |
|---|---|
| Henry Khoo | Henry Khoo |
| QF 223  10:45 AM | QF 223 |
| Gate: 67  Seat: 17B | 10:45 AM |
| Please proceed to the boarding gate 60 minutes before departure time. | Gate: 67 |
| | Seat: 17B |

"I have to catch up to my parents!" I snatch my pass and run toward my pretend mom and dad.

The airline staffer is still watching me. I'm not safe yet. "Mommy! Daddy!" I call out.

Luckily, that seems to convince the airline staffer. She turns to another person.

But my "daddy" turns around to me. He squints at me and asks, "Did you call us Mommy and Daddy?"

Uh . . . I'm on the phone. A very important phone call—

RRRRIIIIING!

YIKES!

Bao Bao, why is it so noisy over at Pheebs's house?

JI-JIE!

 You're not doing anything dangerous, are you?

 That's just an online video. We're doing some research for the project.

 Good. I don't want anyone to get hurt. Popo asked me to tell you something because she is allergic to learning how to text. She said,

"金隆，这部电视剧好精彩! 那个徒弟就快要赴汤蹈火!" (Henry, this TV drama is exciting! The disciple is about to swim across boiling water and tread through fire!)

 That sounds dangerous. Anyway, don't call me! Text me! Bye!

Popo is way too obsessed with wuxia, interrupting my fake school project just to tell me about that disciple. Maybe she's the one who needs to grow up. But like the disciple in her show, I am about to swim across boiling water and tread through fire.

My next destination is the airside area of the airport, which is a part only passengers with boarding passes, in addition to passports, can enter. It's like the villain's lair in wuxia dramas. In the middle of this lair lies the ultimate wisdom. To enter the villain's lair, first I need to survive the very, very treacherous Realm of Trials.

I march forward. The Realm of Trials will be treacherous, but judging by Tim Aditya's smirk, he has probably outed me to Principal Trang. Rather than suffering the consequences of everyone finding out I'm Fly on the Wall, I'd much rather swim across boiling water and tread through fire.

# Realm of Trials

## TRIAL 1: X-RAY SCANNER ENTRANCE

Usually, my family takes my bag from me and puts it through the first trial. Today I follow the signs that tell me what I can't bring into the airside area.

security staff

all liquids more than 3 oz.

## TRIAL 2: WALK THROUGH THE METAL DETECTOR

I sail through the detector, but it beeps for the man behind me. The security staffer hovers the metal-detecting wand all over him, and it beeps at the right side of his face. "This happens every time I fly," he says, "My jaws are faulty, so part of them has been replaced by metal." He fishes out a letter from his doctor explaining this, and the security staffer lets him go.

If only there were such things as fault-detecting wands. A surgeon could remove those parts of me that are faulty and replace them with normal ones.

**TRIAL 3: X-RAY SCANNER EXIT**

You should hold your boarding pass and ticket instead of leaving them in the tray. You could have lost them.

Did you pack your bag yourself?

Have you got anything in here that shouldn't be here?

?!?

What could the illegal thing in my bag possibly be? Did my family sneak in something else that I missed? A Tupperware of fried chicken with lots of gravy? A thermos of herbal chicken soup? A seven-course meal? They must have done it on the one-in-a-million chance that Pheebs's dads would be a second late to serve lunch to Bao Bao.

But turns out, I'd forgotten something very important inside the first aid kit.

a pair of scissors for cutting bandages

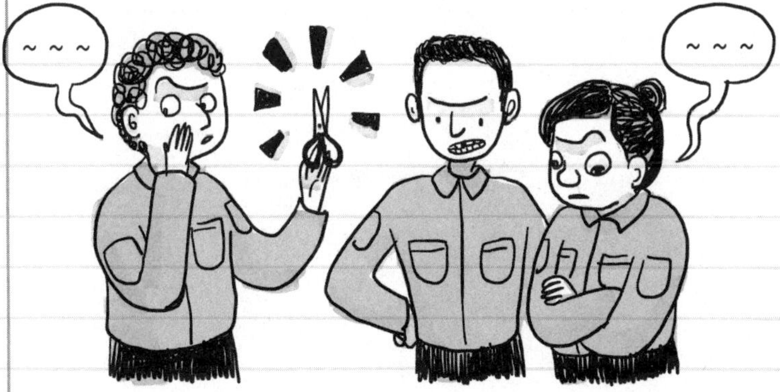

Are more security staff going to swarm out and arrest me? Will they drag me in front of a judge?

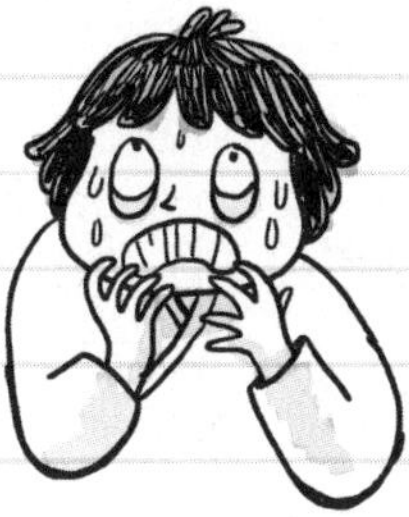

I'll beg for a fine instead of jail time with scar-faced bad guys. But I can only afford $396.90 in fines. I'll beg the judge to accept an IOU.

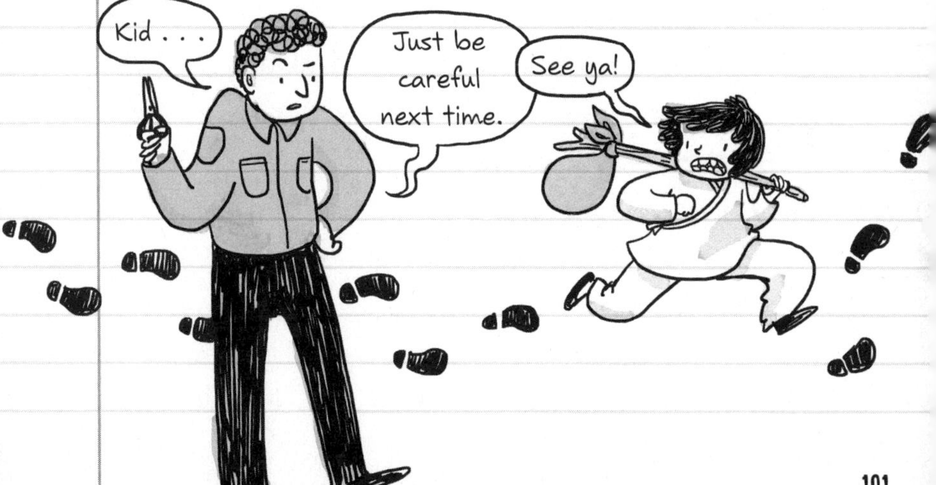
Kid . . .
Just be careful next time.
See ya!

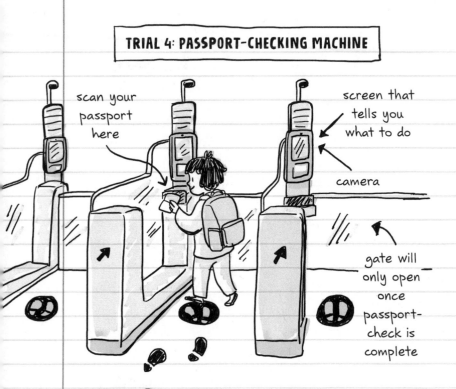

## TRIAL 4: PASSPORT-CHECKING MACHINE

scan your passport here

screen that tells you what to do

camera

gate will only open once passport-check is complete

Popo hates these machines. She prefers the time in history when passports were checked by humans. She's old school. She thinks DVD players work by magic. Whenever I suggest that she could watch even more wuxia dramas on Netflix, she pats the DVD player and says, "老马识途。" (An old horse knows the way.) If you're confused, join the club. Popo likes to use Chinese proverbs and idioms created by ancient and dead old men to confuse us so she'll have the last say.

Today I hate these machines, too. The gate refuses to open.

The screen orders me to seek help at a manned desk at the left. When I get there, I hand my passport to the immigration officer. He scans my passport on a little machine on his desk. And then . . .

This is it. My family has discovered my plan and called the police. My passport has been flagged as YOU SHALL NOT PASS. Like if a wanted criminal is trying to flee the country. Or maybe the security staff at Trial 3 texted him all about my scissors smuggling.

"Is this you in this passport photo?" the immigration officer barks.

Ye-Yes! That photo was taken half a year ago. I'm an inch taller now. Who else could it be?

An evil twin? A clone?

A hologram?

Ha ha.

Or is it because you can't recognize me because I wasn't smiling in the passport photo? I'll frown.

No, no, I wasn't frowning in my passport. I had a neutral expression.

Sweat patches bloom on my underarms. The immigration officer plops my passport back on the desk. Still not smiling, and barely moving his lips, he grumbles, "It was just a routine question." And then he goes into complete silence again, just staring at me.

I look away. In dog language, looking into another dog's eyes is rude and could spark fights.

Finally, he spares my life. "You can go, you know."

"Woof!" I say, and scamper away.

Emerging from the Realm of Trials in sweet victory!

My family has been making me carry that first aid kit since December, but I completely forgot about the scissors, since I've never needed to use the kit. Mom said, "Just in case."

"Accidents happen," Jie added.

Obviously, she was referring to the bicycle accident, but she made it sound like it was my fault. Little does she know that she and Mom and Popo tailgating me not only caused the accident, but also brought about Step 2 in Henry Khoo's transformation into Fly on the Wall.

That day, it was pure luck that I'd cycled far enough so no one at that party witnessed me wipe out. I didn't see Pheebs again for the rest of the break because she went to visit her grandparents outside of Perth. I spent the remaining weeks staring out the window watching other kids play. I didn't mind it as much as my family, who signed me up for two after-school classes—Poetry for Kids and Digital Art for Kids. If there was any opportunity for me to make more friends, my family would sniff it out and snatch it up for me.

I didn't end up gaining new friends, but I gained new skills, one of which came in handy as Fly on the Wall.

At Digital Art for Kids, I was taught to explore new drawing styles by copying my favorite artists. I decided to mimic the style in Pheebs's and my favorite graphic novel, *HI-YA!*

me in my usual style →

← me in *HI-YA!* style

It took a lot of practice and a little encouragement from Popo before I grasped it, and I ended up using it to create Fly on the Wall comics. It is so different from my usual drawing style that even Pheebs couldn't guess that I'm Fly on the Wall.

I didn't know it then, how things happened one after the other, leading to my eventual transformation into Fly on the Wall, but looking back, it began this way:

## HENRY KHOO'S TRANSFORMATION
## INTO FLY ON THE WALL

Step 1: My family tailgating me at Pheebs's birthday party.

Step 2: My family forcing me to attend Digital Art for Kids.

NEW
shark hat

monkey
backpack

yellow
raincoat

polka dot
T-shirt

rainbow
leggings

rubber
boots

It looks like
there's a shark
feasting on the
boy's head.

His dad notices me staring and laughs. "My son
picks out his own clothes."

"My dad says I'm a very independent little
person," the boy says, puffing out his chest. With
that, he bounds away, pulling his dad along.

I'm left with my meh clothes and my curious
thoughts.

Hmmm . . .
Every night, my
family picks out the
next day's clothes
for me. They also
pick them out for
me at Kmart.

Do they
choose my
clothes based on
my fashion sense?
Or is my fashion
sense chosen by
them?

Today, that all changes. I'm going to discover my
very own fashion sense.

Metamorphosis "R" Us (clothing store)

The airport is like a mall. There are stores selling everything from giant candy bars to books to key chains to fashion senses. I pick the first store selling kids' clothes. Inside it, the selection is endless. I thought jeans were just jeans, but there are actually skinny ones, straight ones, slim fit ones, and many others—more types than there are dog breeds.

When my family was choosing a dog breed, Jie had the last say, since she was the one who'd been asking for a dog. She decided to get a Brittany spaniel because our neighbor has one. Our neighbor's dog is a *real* dog, the kind of dog you see in books, movies, and TV—friendly, bouncy, waggy-tailed. Even its name, Rover, is a real doggish name.

But Maomi, he's nothing like Rover. He's so undoggish that Jie picked a name for him that means "cat" in Mandarin.

For the past half a year, I've been walking him along the forest tracks while Popo waits nearby, but before that, Jie and I used to walk Maomi at the fenced dog park near our home.

# I MISS MAOMI

When we reached the park, Maomi would greet the other dogs there.

But after he'd said, "Hi!" to the dogs, he'd walk away. And just watch.

Sometimes a dog approached Maomi and they'd play.

But if more dogs joined in . . .

Weird or not, I love Maomi. I miss him.

"May I help you?" the shopkeeper asks, snapping me out of missing Maomi.

I point to a mannequin at the center of the store. Whatever it's wearing must be the *in* look. Too bad my school has uniforms. If I wore this *in* outfit to school, maybe I wouldn't be so *out*. I'd be one of the party-hat rats at the cheese party, instead of the laboratory-coat scientist observing them.

"Very stylish," the shopkeeper says. "The fitting room's right there."

Being in a fitting room on my own for the first time isn't as exciting as expected. But as I'm taking off my shirt, I experience another first that's the opposite of meh. It's so WOWZA! it brings out the poet in me like a burp.

Oh, you've finally arrived.
You are wispy and light brown,
not like what I expected.
You mark the end of my babyhood,
which is what my adventure is all about.
Oh, you've finally arrived.
I've been waiting for you for so long,
my first underarm hair.

Hey, don't mock my poem
that doesn't follow poetry's many rules
like assonance, haiku, and tanka.
My poet-teacher told me to write
whatever I wanted,
however I wanted, and
*if what you write lets you see the invisible things,*
*then it's a good poem.*
So don't mock my poem,
because soon I'll have magic eyes.

If my poet-teacher read my Ode to Underarm Hair,
he'd probably ask,

*What does it let you see?*
*I'd answer,*
*That I'm a weird kid*
*who writes poems about underarm hair.*

If Dad were here, maybe I could ask him how long it'll take for my underarm hair to be impressively dark like his, which I saw when we went swimming at the pool in his apartment complex. (I don't go around studying people's armpits, cross my heart.) That would give us something to talk about with multiple long sentences. Other questions to keep our conversation going would be: When will the forest in my armpits really come in? And when washing underarm hair, do I use body lotion, shampoo, and/or conditioner?

I couldn't ask these questions during our family's weekly video call because these questions are private. In my home, finding privacy is like searching for a kid who loves homework.

Maybe all along, somewhere deep down in its wrinkles, my brain knew that I had to go on this adventure. Not just to gain wisdom from a shifu and prove my independence, but also to ask Dad these questions. Maybe I've always had some nuggets of wisdom inside me, but I just don't know it. It's like Maomi being surprised by his own fart.

Sometimes, when you least expect it, something comes out of you that you didn't even know was in you.

I want to study my first underarm hair more, but . . .

Final call for passengers Anita Kumar, Vinai Kumar, Chingyuan Chen, Chingtan Chen, and Evelyn Herron.

Please proceed to your boarding gate immediately.

Phew! Not my flight.

Oh, and passenger Henry Khoo.

!

I stuff myself into the rest of the new clothes. It slipped my mind that I'm in a rush. My family usually keeps me on schedule with school, meals, showers, bedtime, and all other activities. Even things that should be totally private, like my bathroom time.

*Henry, you haven't pooped since yesterday. Let's have bran for breakfast!*

My new clothes fit like a glove.

THE NEW, IMPROVED HENRY!

vest I picked out myself

shirt I picked out myself

"skinny" breed jeans I picked out myself

boots I picked out myself

The New, Improved Henry zooms off. Wait for me, Pilot!

But someone grabs my backpack. I'm yanked backward. I've only gotten as far as several steps out of the store. Oh no! I'm being kidnapped! Just like Jie said I would! My adventure is over, and the worst thing about it is that Jie was right!

I can't let the list of Consequences of Henry Khoo's Jailbreak come true. I twist myself free of my backpack. Turns out, my kidnapper is the shopkeeper of Metamorphosis "R" Us. He grabs my arm. "You're not going anywhere but my store. I'm calling your parents and security."

How does he know that I'm on an illegal adventure? "I have a good explanation! I need to prove that I'm not a baby!"

"And you think this is the right way?" He uses that adult tone that means he's going to answer his own question. "New clothes do not make you a grown-up."

"Oh. I didn't mean

Nor does shoplifting.

Metamorphosis "R" Us Maximum Security Jail

In some of Popo's wuxia shows, there are monks.
Some of them are allies who will help the lone
wanderers, but some are evil. Both types possess
far-out martial arts prowess, which can help or
hinder the disciple.

Pete the storekeeper
is like one of those
monks. And from the
way Monk Pete is
squinting and frowning
at me, my bet is he's
the evil type.

I squirm under Monk Pete's glare. The hems of
my new "stolen" vest poke me through my new shirt.
I don't dare scratch. As an arrested criminal, I know
I'm allowed one phone call, but I'm not sure if I have
the right to scratch myself everywhere like a monkey.

I don't know which is worse—my parents being
called up because I'm an underage adventurer or
because I'm a shoplifter. Either way, I only have
one reaction:

I'm sorryI'msorryI'msorry
I'msorry. I forgot to pay
because I'm going to be
late for my flight. You see,
I'm on this adventure to
prove my independence! I
can pay, I swear!

Monk Pete crosses his arms and leans back to place his weight on one leg. That's what adults do to make themselves comfortable to listen to a kid's lengthy excuse about whatever trouble they caused. If I want him to let me go, I have to spill.

I shuffle on my feet. My new boots pinch a little.

At my best friend's birthday party last semester break, there was an accident. It only happened because my family babied me. When school started again in January, I thought my best friend was going to still be mad, but she wasn't. Except when recess came, she didn't want to sit at our usual table, just the two of us, like we always did since kindergarten. She said, *We should sit at that table with Dee and the others.*

If only my teachers were here now to listen to me speaking up more. It doesn't come naturally to me, like drawing. I pick up a pencil and I can just draw without really thinking. The only reason I could say all these words without going ummm ahhh ehhh is because these thoughts about Pheebs have played over and over in my mind for a long time. It's as if I'm a cow and information is grass.

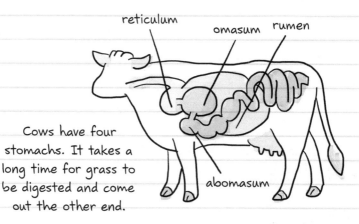

reticulum
omasum
rumen
abomasum

Cows have four stomachs. It takes a long time for grass to be digested and come out the other end.

Except that in my case, what comes out the other end smells nicer. They are thoughts that I can write down and express in actual words.

"And?" Monk Pete demands.

"I'm not a dictator. I didn't stop her from sitting at that table. And I didn't really mind sitting with the others." My "skinny" jeans wrap around my legs too tightly. My new clothes actually fit me like a glove. I should have picked another breed of jeans. Maybe the Totally Chill breed.

Pete rubs his shiny head. "Then . . . what's wrong?"

"I . . . don't understand why she wanted to make more friends—" I choke. Those words that just came out of my mouth sound so selfish. I don't want to be a selfish kid. Except I am. A better kid wouldn't have such thoughts pop into his head. My nose warns me that I might bawl my eyes out in five Mississippi, four Mississippi, three Mississippi . . . I shake my legs to distract myself.

"What's wrong with making more friends?" Monk Pete asks.

"Nothing." I can't bring myself to say these other even more selfish words that are burning the tip of my tongue.

Maybe
I wasn't enough,
like she was
enough to me.

Monk Pete shifts to lean on his other foot. He's not satisfied with my answer.

I continue. "And then—And then—" At that moment, I realize what Step 3 in Henry Khoo's Transformation into Fly on the Wall was. It was Pheebs and me sitting at that table with the other kids.

Though I wasn't sure why Pheebs and I needed to sit with anyone else, those kids actually turned out to be interesting. They talked about everything under the sun, from Austin's favorite band, Perfect Ones, to Dee's mom's homemade gulab jamun to the possum that lives in Yangmei's roof. And I'd thought Pheebs and I knew everything about each other, but turned out, I hadn't known that she had recently taken up guitar or that she was thinking of trying out for the swim team.

Hanging out with other kids was different, but it was a good kind of different, like the tight outlines in *HI-YA!* versus the looser outlines in my drawing. They were both great.

Pete pulls up a stool from behind the rack of jeans and plops himself down. "And then what happened?"

"A boy named Tim Aditya happened."

Dee invited Tim to sit at the table too. I scooted over, and he sat down next to me. The only thing he said throughout the whole lunch was: *I'm not.* That was his answer to Austin's comment: *You're so shy, Tim.*

Then, Yangmei piped up. *Tim's not shy. He's quiet. Just like Henry. Tim and Henry are twins.*

She didn't say it like it was a harmless joke, but like it was a truth, a fact that had been taught in textbooks forever. Like *the world is round.*

*Gravity is real.*

*One human year is equivalent to seven dog years.*

*Tim and Henry are twins.*

Everyone turned to look at me. They said, *I never noticed it before. Oh. Ooooh!*

It's like what happened at the dog park one day. This dog came into the park:

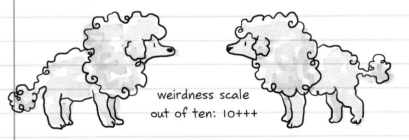

weirdness scale out of ten: 2

A couple of people did a double take. And then another dog came into the park.

weirdness scale out of ten: 10+++

Everyone in the park did double takes. And sniggered.

Maybe I was a poodle with a weird haircut, but no one noticed until Tim the poodle who also had a weird haircut came along.

THE WEIRDOGS

I was annoyed at Austin and Yangmei for saying we were twins, but I was mega-annoyed at Tim for sitting down and being so weird. I know it's not his fault, but knowing is logical, like math—1 plus 1 is always 2. Feeling is not logical, like languages—English has "noses that run" and "feet that smell."

Mostly, I felt astronomically betrayed by Pheebs. She should have banged her fists on the table and yelled, "HENRY IS NOTHING LIKE TIM!" What she did was stab her celery stick into the hummus. Stab stab stab. Like she wished I was the hummus and she was murdering me for embarrassing her with my quiet.

Tim never sat at that table after that, but it was too late. Suddenly the chatter of those other kids turned from interesting trivia to ear-piercing squawks.

Being microchipped as a weird poodle wouldn't have been so bad, if everyone at that table were at least of the canine species.

Shortly after that, I stopped sitting at that table.

Looking back now, I realize that Step 4 in Henry Khoo's Transformation into Fly on the Wall happened when Tim Aditya sat at that table with the chatty magpies.

# FLY ON THE WALL

**MAGPIES SWOOP IN ON CHATSWOOD SCHOOL**

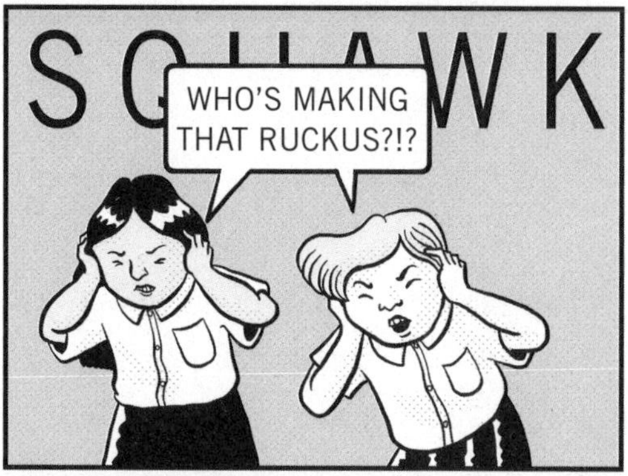
SQUAWK
WHO'S MAKING THAT RUCKUS?!?

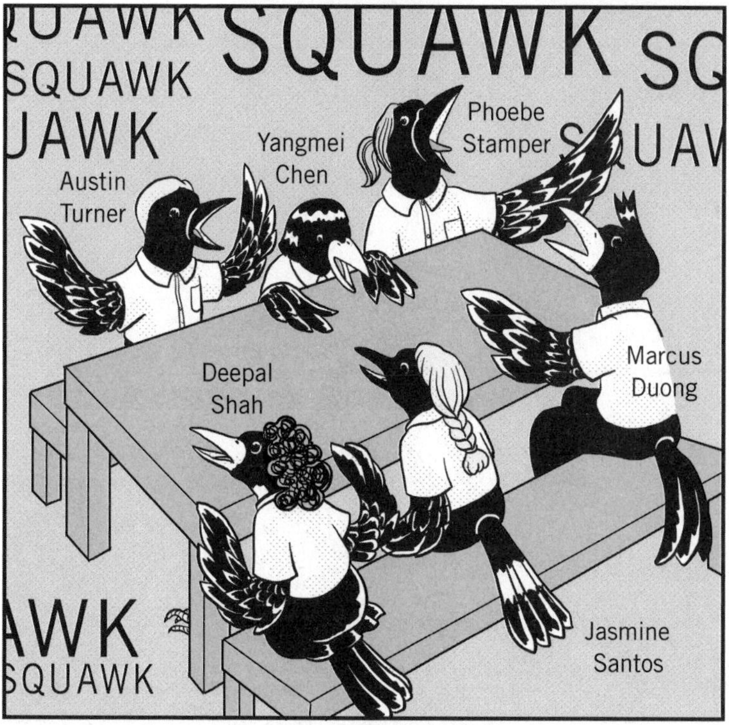
SQUAWK
SQUAWK
SQUAWK
Austin Turner
Yangmei Chen
Phoebe Stamper
Marcus Duong
Deepal Shah
Jasmine Santos
SQUAWK

Metamorphosis "R" Us Supreme Court

I spill everything to Monk Pete, except about my
transformation into Fly on the Wall. He'd convict me
of gossiping on top of shoplifting. "I just ran into
Tim Aditya," I add. "Seeing him reminded me of all
those . . . those . . ." The tears pooling in my eyes
might spill out. I tip my head back. "Nice ceiling."

Monk Pete springs to his feet and marches
behind the counter. That's it. The adventure is over.
He's going to unleash his evil monk superpower—
calling security, or making me call Mom.

"One hundred and sixty," he says.

Do you mean
days? Or years?

Either way, I can't go
to jail for that long!

I have to
walk my
dog.

126

He sighs. "I've had my share of friendship troubles, too. Pay for these new clothes and continue your adventure. Or you could just return them."

There is no time to get out of these clothes. I hand Pete two hundred dollars in cash, and he raises his eyebrows.

Yes, I am Henry Moneybags. And I worked hard for it.

During Chinese New Year, when red packets of cash are given out to younger relatives as gifts, I'm in Perth because school's still in session. My married aunts, uncles, and cousins are nice enough to set the red packets aside until I visit them in Singapore during summer break. In order to get these red packets into my hands, I have to silently suffer all kinds of torture.

How cute!

Gugu (Dad's sister)

Pete hands me my change.

"You . . . ," I say. "You're a good monk."

He huffs. "Just because I'm bald, you think I'm a monk?"

I clamp a hand over my mouth.

But he rubs his head and grins. "Giving advice is not my forte. But I think friends are like fashion. Some are in vogue forever, like a simple white T-shirt, but others go in and out of style, like denim overalls. And then there are items like harem pants that you once thought you'd rather be dead than be caught wearing, but . . ."

Surprise. Surprise. They're very comfortable.

You're running out of time if you want to catch your flight. I shall pray for your safe journey.

With the monk's blessing, I hurry out of the shop and continue on my adventure.

THERE YOU ARE!

Why did you run off on your own?

bluish green jacket of an airline staffer

Jie must have discovered I'm not at Pheebs's, figured it all out, and contacted the airport.

The New, Improved Henry will never get taken out of the box. He'll be forever sealed inside his house by his family.

"Your parents would be very worried if you got lost," the airline staffer says.

I fight a very strong urge to stomp my feet. "I won't get lost!"

The airline staffer reaches toward me.

I duck.

Her hand shoots past me. "Don't leave my side again. Got that, Anita?" She grabs the shoulder of a little girl I just realized is standing behind me. At this moment, five more kids arrive.

That's when I notice that the ID badge hanging from the airline staffer's lanyard says UNACCOMPANIED MINORS PROGRAM ESCORT.

I'm a professor in the subject of Unaccompanied Minors Program. Jie once told us all about this program. That was when she wanted to be a flight attendant, which was after she wanted to be a pilot, which was after she wanted to be a dog trainer, which was before she wanted to be a circus performer, which was all before she wanted to be a vet.

Jie told me that on most airlines, kids under twelve who fly without an adult have to be accompanied by an airline staffer from the check-in point right up until they're picked up at their destination country.

I just made the cutoff age to fly on my own. When a bird pooped on my head on my birthday a few months ago, Popo said it meant good luck. Turns out, she's right, and she is knowledgeable about some things.

I pity these kids in the Unaccompanied Minors Program. It's really just a nice way of saying Official Babies Program. And "escort" is a nice way of saying Official Babysitter. I know how these Official Babies must feel.

Hang in there.

?

one of the Official Babies

"We're already late, kids," the Official Babysitter says. "Let's hurry to the boarding gate!"

"We're late because Chingyuan locked himself in the toilet," the boy standing next to me whispers, as if I've been his BFF forever, and not a stranger. He points to another boy who must be Chingyuan. Anita and Chingyuan—I think those names were mentioned with my name earlier for the last call. The Official Babies are on my flight. "He couldn't unlock the door for a looooong time. By the way, I'm Vinai."

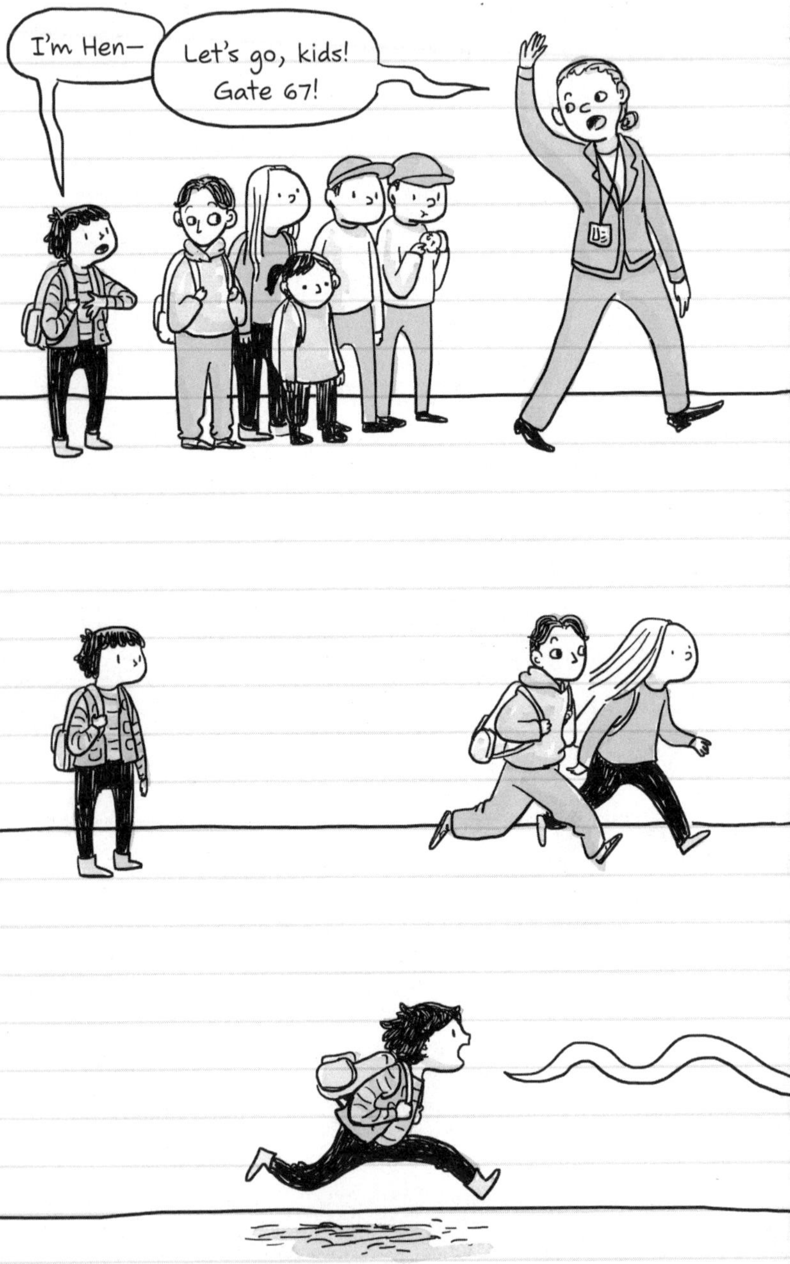
I'm Hen—
Let's go, kids! Gate 67!

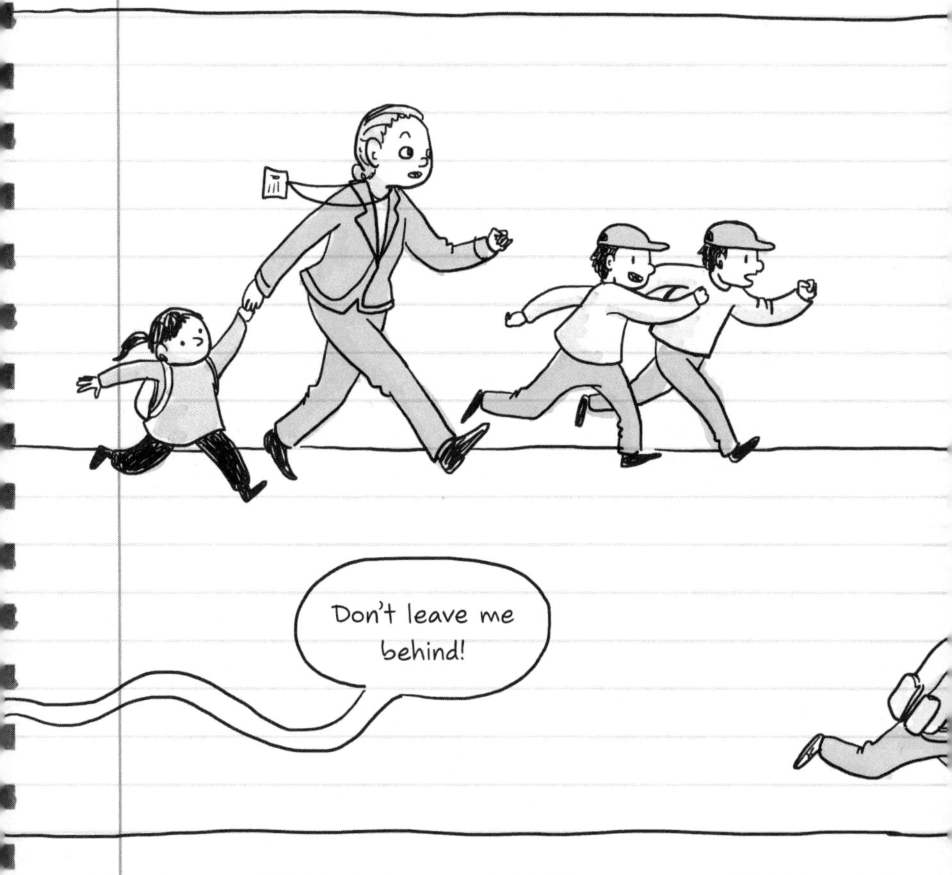
Don't leave me behind!

## COUNTDOWN TO FLIGHT

| 0 | 0 | 2 | 9 |
|---|---|---|---|
| HOURS | | MINUTES | |

Zooming through the airport, weaving through the crowd toward gate 67

I mentioned that I'm of medium speed, but maybe I'm actually turtle speed, because the Official Babies and the Official Babysitter pull farther and farther away from me. It's not 100 percent my fault, though. My boots pinch my toes, and my jeans squeeze my thighs, and the vest scratches my chest. This must be what Jie means by "dressed to kill." I'm so uncomfortable I might die. But if this is what it takes to be *in*, then I'm all in!

The Official Babies reach a moving walkway. Foolishly, they do not hop onto it. Instead, they run alongside the walkway.

I'm wiser, though. I leap onto the moving walkway and it's like I've turned into a

With the moving walkway, I not only catch up to the Official Babies, but overtake them. I get so far ahead of the Official Babies that when I reach gate 67 and turn back, they're still nowhere to be seen.

The gate is not actually a gate but a room.

my airplane

a giant hamster tunnel connects the "gate" to the airplane

glass wall

go in here to enter the giant hamster tunnel.

On second thought, I should speak like an adult since I have underarm hair. Correction: The room is connected to the airplane by a skybridge.

I join the short line of people waiting to board the plane. In no time, I'm traipsing down the skybridge.

Stepping off the skybridge, I find myself at the front of the plane, in the Business Class section. Here, each seat is like the royal throne. It's so wide I could sit in it, extend both hands, and not come into contact with a family member. It must feel like:

Please keep a respectable distance from His Majesty.

That's what I imagine anyway. I've never sat in this section.

When I was purchasing my ticket online, I could have picked a Business Class seat, but while I mentioned that I'm rich, I'm not $4,457.13 rich. Perth to Singapore flights are usually about $400, but there was a big First Day of School Break sale.

I continue on to 17B, my Economy Class seat.

My seatmate is not a shifu with a beard like snow.

She reminds me of Mom. If she's anything like Mom, any wisdom she imparts to me will be something along the lines of *good manners are free, each grain of rice that you leave on your plate will be a pimple on your face, always listen to your mom.*

I buckle myself in and fish my phone out. It's time to gloat.

**JIE**
**WETALK**

I'm having fun, Jie! Making many good friends. I haven't gotten lost or gotten a cold or gotten myself killed.

You're too little for sarcasm.
Have you killed anybody, though?

Ha. Ha. Very funny.

I've made it all this way on my own. All I'm waiting for is my

Shifu!

Finally! I'm about to gain the ultimate wisdom that will fix everything in my life. What will it be? Buy a new bicycle for Pheebs, and she will be your sworn sister again. Eat five servings of broccoli a day for seven nights and become the perfect son and brother. Get bitten by a mutant spider, and you'll be strong and quick and always win the fight in the end.

But there's already someone sitting next to me. "Shifu, what's your seat number?" I ask.

He holds up his boarding pass and points to the seat number: 17B.

Strange. That's my seat. I show him my boarding pass.

He points to the flight number on my boarding pass: QF223. He then points to the flight number on his boarding pass: QF229.

Kid . . .

You're on the wrong flight.

Henry Khoo, Henry Khoo, you ruin everything.

How did you enter gate 69 instead of 67 and get on the wrong plane? Don't blame anyone else. Yes, the machine that scans boarding passes at gate 69 was broken, and the airline staff at gate 69 didn't check your pass properly.

Still, a responsible, independent kid wouldn't have entered the wrong gate.

Henry Khoo, Henry—

AH-CHOO!

Uh-oh.

WET

Henry Khoo, Henry Khoo, your mom and sister are right. The Consequences of Henry Khoo's Jailbreak are coming true.

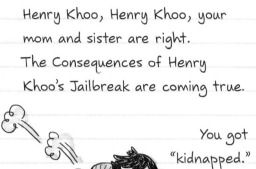

You got "kidnapped." You got "lost." You got a cold.

Your eyes were misty so many times.

You are helpless. You are useless. You are always less, never more.

Gate 67, the right gate for the right flight

The missing passenger. Henry Khoo.

She says my name the way my teacher calls out Austin who's always passing notes to Yangmei in class. "If you're traveling on your own," she adds, "you need to be responsible like a grown-up. You need to be at the gate an hour before the flight. And you need to not get lost."

My legs tremble as I hurry down the skybridge into the plane—the right plane. Three things on Mom and Jie's list of Consequences of Henry Khoo's Jailbreak have come true. The fourth thing is that I will cry, and I'm still struggling with that. The fifth thing is that I will get hurt.

Maybe I'll accidentally cut a big blood vessel when I'm buttering the bread roll that comes with the plane meal. Maybe I'll accidentally fall into the

toilet midair and accidentally flush myself and be
sucked down and ejected out of the plane. Maybe
I'll land in a big grassy field and miraculously survive,
only to be accidentally trampled by cows.

When I enter the plane, I immediately discover
how I'll get hurt.

That's the passenger who got lost.

He delayed all of us. How could such a little kid travel alone?

I'll be stabbed to death by the cutting stares of
the Business Class passengers.

All I can do is concentrate on my fashionable new
boots and hurry down the aisle. But at row 17, seat
A is taken by the little boy with the unique fashion
sense. Sitting next to him is his dad.

I can't believe I boarded the wrong plane again!

Where am I going to end up? The North Pole? I'd definitely catch a cold there.

Before I can turn around and march off yet another wrong plane, a flight attendant appears at my side. "There was a mistake, and this gentleman and his young son were seated separately. Would you mind swapping and sitting at 19B instead?"

"But does this flight go to Singapore?"

The attendant nods, and I'm so relieved I wouldn't care even if the attendant told me that my seat is the toilet. Maybe it's fate, or Popo's deities have decided to take pity on me, and my new seatmate will turn out to be my shifu.

But when I get to my row . . .

Ah! It's you!

The one with the weird sense of humor.

My name's Norleena. But you can call me Nor.

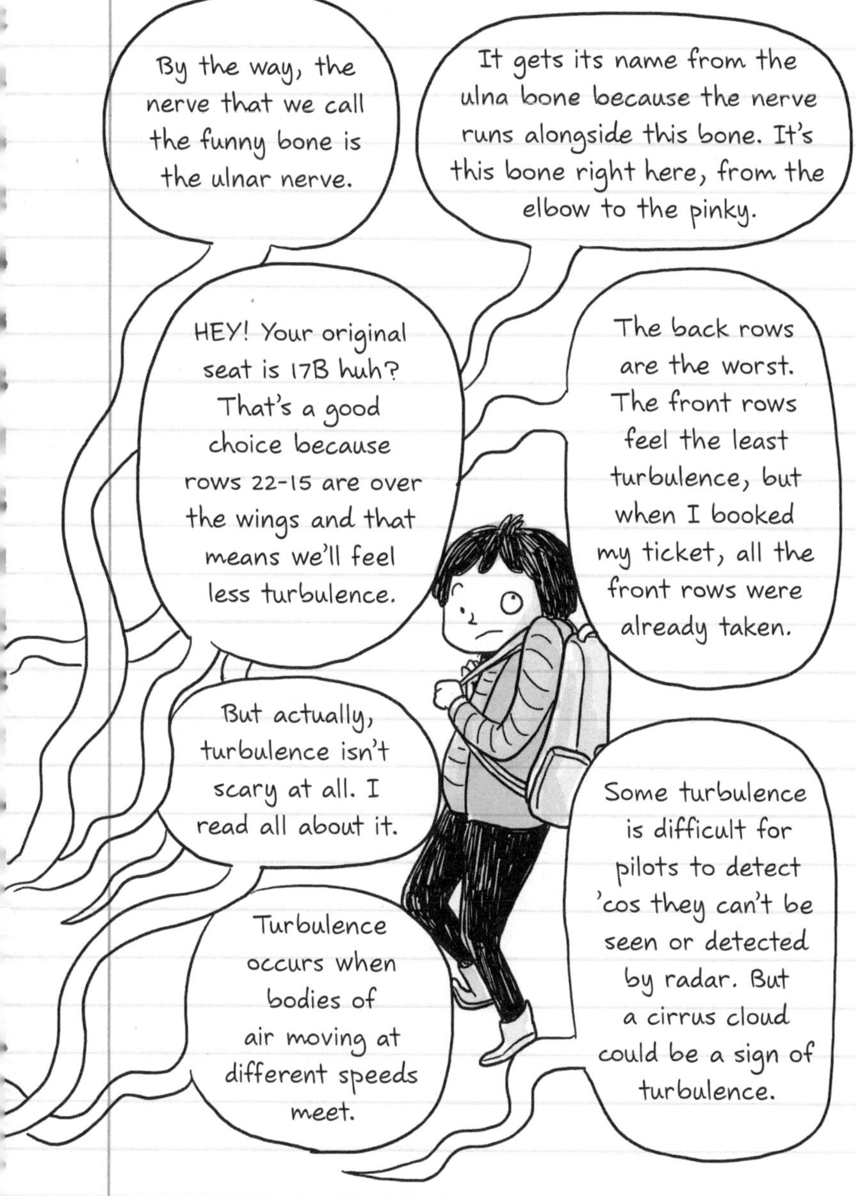


Instead of a shifu, I get a talking Wikipedia.

I sit and place my backpack at my feet. Nor's dad and mom don't seem to be sitting nearby.

Nor points at my backpack. "You're supposed to stow your bag under the seat in front of you. Otherwise when there's an emergency, you and I are going to trip on it."

I do as she says, even though I already knew the rule and was about to do exactly that.

"What's your name?" She swings her legs up and down so vigorously my seat shakes. "What are you writing in that book?"

"My name's Henry. And it's private."

She's quiet. Just for a second. "You have to put on your seat belt."

I clip my seat belt and mutter, "The plane's not even moving yet."

She points at the lit seat belt sign above us.

Instead of a shifu, I'm stuck with a bossy rule-stickler for the next five hours. What's worse is that Nor is probably only a little older than me. Being bossed by another kid makes you the biggest baby ever.

"The attendants gave these out before you got here." She shoves a small packet of mixed nuts and a sealed cup of water toward me. "I made sure to get one for the person who will be my friend for the next five hours."

Friend? I could use one. "Thanks."

"Are you flying with your mom and dad? Where are they?"

"Uh . . ." I don't know her well enough to be sure she won't tattle to a flight attendant and get me kicked off the flight.

"Or are you flying on your own too?"

"Too?"

Nor adjusts her seat belt for the millionth time. "Uh-huh. I'm on my own."

A FELLOW ADVENTURER! "How old are you?"

"Turned twelve last week."

Turns out I'm older, even if only by a few months. "What's the lie you told your parents so they'd let you get on a plane by yourself?"

"What? I told them the truth, that I wanted to visit my cousins. My parents can't come 'cos they have to work. They bought a ticket for me—it was on sale!—and they saw me off at the airport."

That's it. Parallel universes exist, and Nor and I

are witnessing a scientific phenomenon where two of those worlds meet. She lives in the other universe, a storybook universe where parents let kids go on adventures alone and don't make lists of Consequences of Jailbreak. Maybe she even got mail from Hogwarts.

She points at me. "HEY! Does that mean you lied to your parents—"

"I never lie!" I lie. "I'm just surprised. Most of my friends' parents are helicopter parents."

Nor nods many times, slowly. "When my friend Jessica takes the ten-minute bus ride to my house, her dad tracks her location using her phone. And my friend Jingwen, who is a great baker, is only allowed to use the hot oven when his mom is around. Unbelievable!"

Totally. I cannot believe Nor's friends are even allowed to do those things in the first place. Jie would have insisted on riding the bus with me, and Mom would have baked the cake for me. But Nor doesn't need to know the harsh facts of my life. I ask instead, "How many friends do you have?"

I've never counted. There's Jingwen, Ed, Ben, Tim, Sun, Kai . . .

If my family didn't baby me, would it be easier to make friends?

If I were allowed to be independent, would I have as many friends as Nor does? Instead of zero?

I stuff the packet of mixed nuts into the little pocket on my vest, which feels even stiffer now. No more eating snacks that are the optimum size to be lodged in my throat.

While Nor prattles off something about the Heimlich maneuver, I think about how maybe my family is right to baby me: When I do things on my own, I somehow always end up hurting myself.

Bao Bao was not allowed to eat crusty toast because he might choke.
So he lied lied lied.
Now here his corpse lies lies lies
Under this stone
With a nut stuck in his throat.

If I don't get off this plane, those are the words that might be on my tombstone.

On the plane, seat 19B

Mom and Jie's list of Consequences of Henry Khoo's Jailbreak should be called Deadly Accurate Fortune-teller Predictions about Bao Bao's Failures. So far, the predictions have been close calls, but I still have a long way to go. What if the next time those things come true, they aren't close calls? The news headlines could be:

THE DAILY NUGGET

BOY GETS HIMSELF LOST. REALLY LOST.

THE DAILY NUGGET

LOST BOY KIDNAPPED BY ALIENS

THE DAILY NUGGET

**KIDNAPPED BOY RELEASED BY ALIENS**

Aliens say, "We are sick of having to do everything for the helpless human boy."

I should get off the plane. I'll hang out somewhere, maybe the dog park, and at five o'clock, I'll wait at Pheebs's front porch for my family to pick me up. I'll pretend I've been at Pheebs's all day long. I just have to be fine with watching all the other kids having fun with their friends this semester break, be fine with being forced to attend more after-school programs to make friends.

And be fine with having Dad not like me.

It's just until I get the chance to prove to him that I'm not a troublesome kid.

This stinks.

BZZZ BZZZZZ!

It's Mom calling. My lips tremble. It's a reflex. Mom has seen me cry so many times that I don't get too embarrassed about breaking down in front of her anymore. Except today I'm trying to prove that I'm not a baby. I pinch my own arm, then I press ACCEPT CALL.

Are you hungry, Henry? I'm coming over with a basket of muffins.

NO! I mean—Thanks, Mom, but we have muffins here.

"Henry, did you know?" Nor says even though I'm on a call. "There's no evidence that portable devices like cell phones interfere with signals between the plane and ground control and cause mishaps, but they decided it's better to be safe than sorry. You can still use your phone on airplane mode. You just have to connect to the plane's in-flight Wi-Fi—"

"Ssshh!" I point out the window and whisper, "The plane is still attached to the skybridge. It's still okay to use our phones."

🧑‍🦱 Is that one of your new friends? What's her name?

🧒 Umm . . . Ah . . . That was just Dee talking. You've met Dee before.

🧑‍🦱 What about your new friends? Maybe they'd like muffins.

🧒 Mom, we're busy. I'll text you later, okay?

🧑‍🦱 Hold on, Henry. Popo wants to talk to you. I'm putting you on speaker.

👵 你在这里陪我看武侠剧就好了。师父在示范很妙的旋风脚。这样转，然后 。。。踢! (If only you were here to watch this wuxia drama with me. The shifu is demonstrating the fantastic Whirlwind Foot. You turn like this, and then . . . KICK!)

👤 Watch it, Popo! You almost got me there!

🧒 婆婆，小心你积水的膝盖! (Popo, be careful with your watery knees!)

Henry! Who are your new best friends?

Shall I bring over cakes? Everyone likes the person whose mom brings cakes.

I'm . . .
I . . .

My family's words blur together, along with my
vision. Their protectiveness of me is annoying, but
right now, it feels like a snuggly blanket I could safely
cry into. My near-death-by-mixed-nuts experience
rattled me so much I'm not thinking straight.

 啊! 谁没关窗户? 有苍蝇飞进屋里了。看, 它就
趴在墙上。我用旋风脚对付它。(Ah! Who didn't
close the window? There's a fly in the house.
Look, it's just perched on the wall. I shall use
Whirlwind Foot to defeat it.)

Haha. Fly on the wall. Like the one on the
internet.

如果那只苍蝇在墙上，它怎么会同时在网里面呢？ (If that fly is on the wall, how could it be caught in the net?)

Popo, "fly on the wall" is an idiom! And it's on the internet, not like *in* a butterfly net. Don't tell me I have to teach you the internet all over again!

Here, Ma, I'll show you Fly on the Wall's blog on my phone, see—Oh! There are weird comments on the most recent post.

Let me see. Hmm . . . These comments were made last night by the same person. Mom, do you think it's Principal Trang?

I doubt it. He's an adult and a school principal. He wouldn't post that.

But who's this person who knows Fly on the Wall's real identity?

!

With trembling hands, I place my family on speaker and open the browser on my phone. I go to flyonthewallatchatswoodschool.saysomethingblog.com.

💬 **Comments** (348)　　　　　　　　　**Comment**

| **Newest** | Oldest |
|---|---|

**Jonjon5**, 2 weeks ago

FLLLYYYY!

Replies (12) | Reply

**FROGINTHEWELL**, 14 hours ago

Reply

**FROGINTHEWELL**, 14 hours ago

Reply

**FROGINTHEWELL**, 14 hours ago

I know who you are.

Reply

**FROGINTHEWELL**, 14 hours ago

The frog is going to catch the fly.

Reply

GASP!

As I fumble to pick up my phone, I accidentally press the HANG UP button.

Nor is staring at me. Her lips are clamped tight, like she's trying very hard to hold back the million things she must blurt out. Luckily, at that point, a flight attendant walks down the aisle making sure all the window shades are drawn up.

Nor nudges hers, even though it's already all the way up. "The shades have to be up during takeoff and landing for several reasons," she tells me as if I've just asked her. "One, if there's an emergency, we can immediately see the conditions outside and plan the evacuation—"

"We have to watch this," I say, pointing to my entertainment screen. Every channel is playing the same video. The airline is making sure all passengers know what to do in case of emergencies.

Nor watches the emergency movie on her screen like it's an Oscar-winning show, which leaves me in peace to think about my own emergency.

## WHO ON EARTH IS FROG IN THE WELL?

Frog in the Well is an idiom describing an ignorant person who cannot see beyond the little circle of sky that is the size of the well's mouth.

Mom's right. Frog in the Well must be someone other than Principal Trang.

Someone who is a weird poodle.

Back in early May, I was at the computer laboratory, making a new post on the *Fly on the Wall* blog. Right after I clicked PUBLISH, I turned . . .

I have no idea how long Tim had been watching my computer. He was a mouse who didn't make a peep. He just looked at me. I didn't move until I heard footsteps approaching the room and Principal Trang out in the hall saying, "Recess is almost over, kids."

I should have whispered to Tim, "If you tell anyone I'm the Fly, you're dead meat," or "If you don't tell, I'll be your butler for a month," but all my excellent responses always come on time for "too late."

Instead, I shoved past Tim and fled. Except my escape didn't go as planned . . .

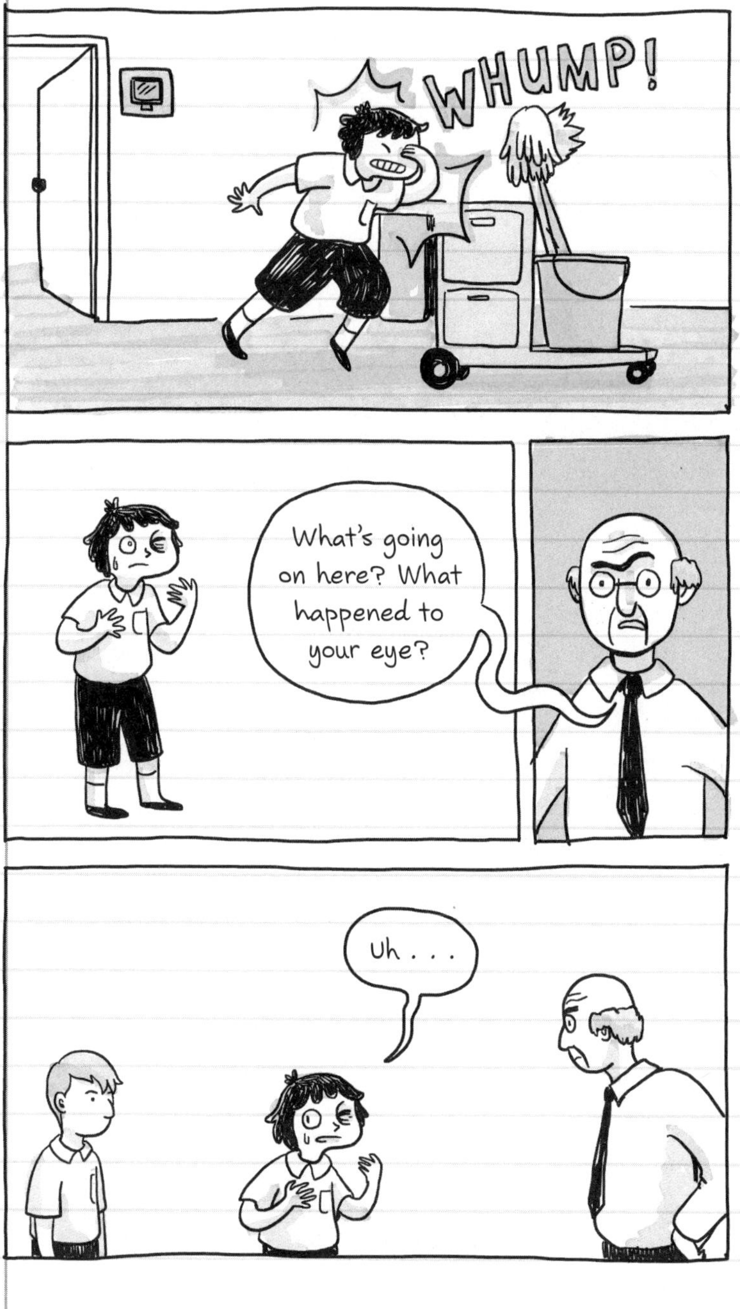
WHUMP!
What's going on here? What happened to your eye?
Uh . . .

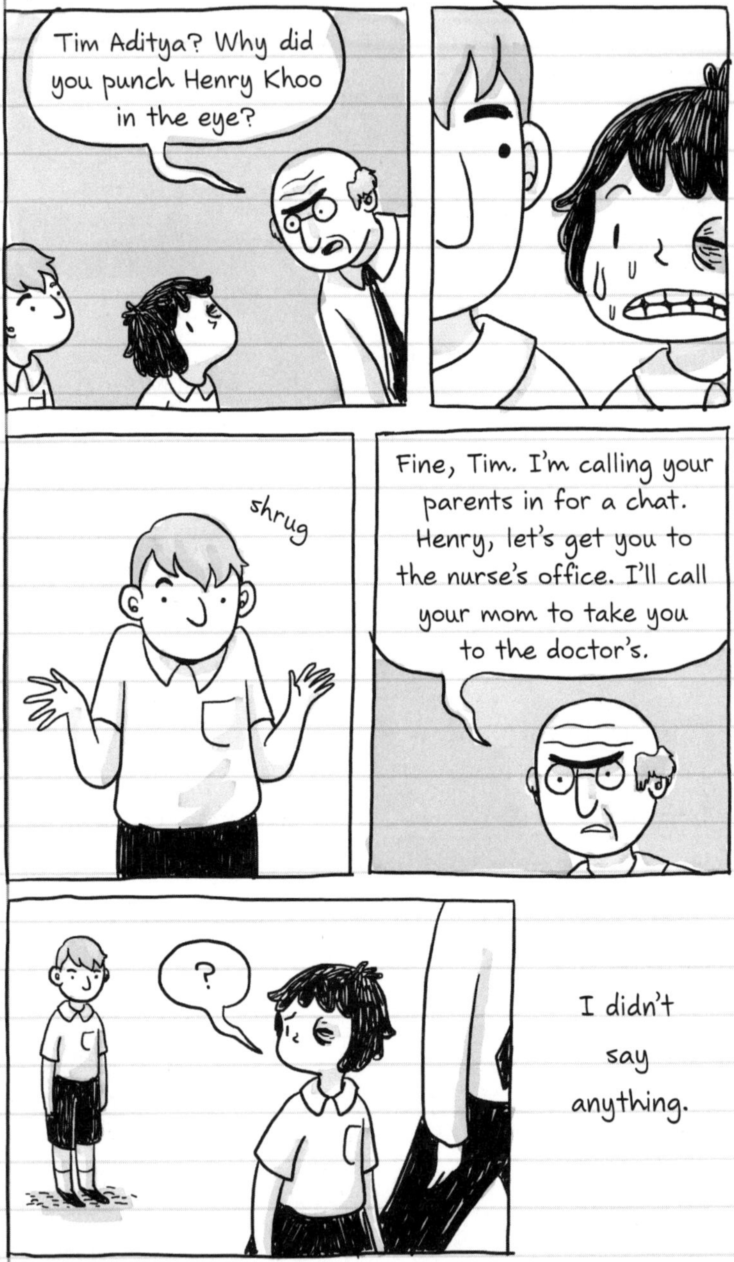
Tim Aditya? Why did you punch Henry Khoo in the eye?
shrug
Fine, Tim. I'm calling your parents in for a chat. Henry, let's get you to the nurse's office. I'll call your mom to take you to the doctor's.
?
I didn't say anything.

I was too stumped by Tim's response and too worried about the eye patch I might have to wear every day from then on.

Later, I heard that Principal Trang gave Tim detention every Friday for the rest of the year. Still, Tim didn't spill. The reason he took the fall for me is one of the universe's unsolved mysteries, alongside why Maomi can't hear Mom yelling for him to come inside but can hear the crinkle of a cheese slice wrapper even while fast asleep. But I shouldn't feel guilty for not volunteering the truth about how I got my black eye. After all, I didn't ask Tim to take the blame, and he's not a robot whose programmer is me.

All along, I didn't know if he was planning to eventually reveal the truth about my identity. Now I'm sure he will. Oh yeah. I'm so sure that we can tattoo this on my arm: Tim Aditya, the Frog in the Well, wants to catch Henry Khoo, the Fly on the Wall.

But what does he have up his sleeve? If he's just going to tell Principal Trang the truth, why did he wait? And why bother to post that comment on the blog? Is he going to start a comics blog titled _Frog in the Well_? A blog dedicated to ugly doodles of me?

All I know is this: Whatever Tim the Frog in the Well has in store, it'd stink to be in Perth when it's revealed that I'm Fly on the Wall.

Principal Trang would give me a scalp massage with his filthy fingers. The cafeteria staff would send me a basket of cupcakes with the ingredients clearly labeled: FLOUR, BRUSSELS SPROUTS (MIN. 95%).

The victims of Fly on the Wall and their friends would toilet paper my house. Or cycle past my house just to roll their eyes at me. Or hold a party on my front lawn and not invite me.

And Pheebs. Pheebs. Pheebs. She'd say that she's not my NRFF, but my N4eva. Nemesis forever.

Mom and Jie would be all *WHY WERE YOU HANGING OUT ALONE IN THE COMPUTER LAB DURING RECESS AND LUNCH BREAKS? WHY DON'T YOU HAVE FRIENDS?*

BZZ!

164

Popo told me to tell you something. You should really teach her how to text so she can text you herself.

YOU teach her.

No thanks. All the time when I was teaching her about the internet, I was tearing my hair out.

Anyway, she said: 这武侠剧的徒弟闯大祸。官府的人在找他，所以他远走高飞。

(Translation: The disciple in this wuxia drama got into big trouble. The magistrate is searching for him, so he runs away.)

That disciple has the right idea.

When Frog in the Well croaks loudly about Fly on the Wall's identity, my life in Perth will be over. In Singapore, all I have to deal with is Dad. He might be mad, but I won't know, because he never shows it when he's mad.

There is only one option: I have to fly far, far away.

Phone switched to airplane mode after another friendly reminder by Norpedia

There are instruction videos for what to do in case of plane emergencies. I wish there was a step-by-step guide for when your nemesis gets a hold of your top secret.

Nor glances my way.

Who's Frog in the Well?

No—No one. It's just an idiom.

"Isn't the idiom a frog under a coconut shell?" Nor asks. "It's a Malay idiom. I can speak a little. Katak di bawah tempurung—frog under a coconut shell."

"I didn't know there's a Malay version. In the English version, the frog is in a well."

"How do you know how to speak Mandarin? I heard you speaking it to your family."

"My grandma taught me. She only speaks to my sister and me in Mandarin, to improve our Mandarin."

Popo always says that if her grandchildren can't speak Mandarin, when she dies, her eyes won't be able to close. Which doesn't make sense, because even if her eyes are open, she won't see anything because there are no lights inside a coffin. But old people have a free pass to spout nonsense.

"It's awesome you can speak two languages fluently. I only know a bit of Malay. My mom says she will teach me more when I'm a little older. She says it's very useful to be able to speak multiple languages."

Speaking more than one language isn't really that useful. Technically, I have more words in my brain than people who speak only one language, but I never know the right ones to say.

Like back at that table with the chatty magpies. After my weirdness was pointed out to everyone, thanks partly to Tim Aditya, I decided to change. I started speaking up. Coincidentally, just after I made that decision, Austin brought up the topic of dogs. My favorite!

I told them how at puppy school, the owners are taught to make their puppies get used to having food and toys taken away from them. Some dogs get possessive and aggressive about these things, so it's better to teach them that having food and toys taken away from them is a good thing.

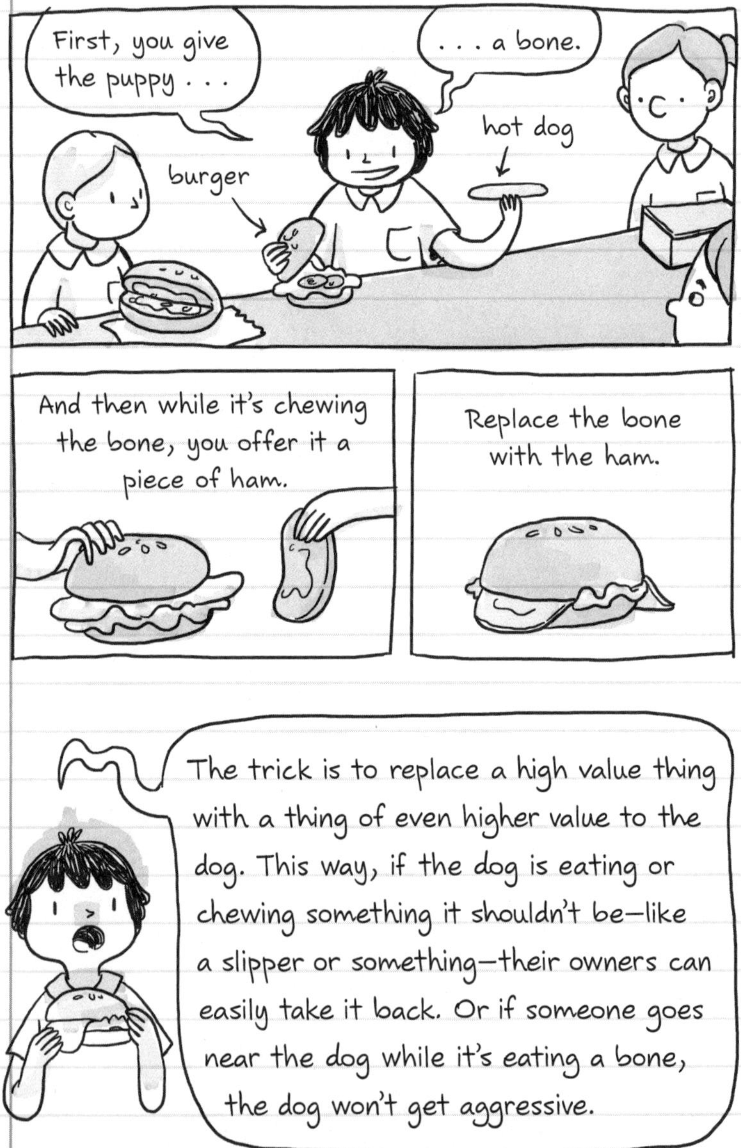
First, you give the puppy . . .
. . . a bone.
burger
hot dog
And then while it's chewing the bone, you offer it a piece of ham.
Replace the bone with the ham.
The trick is to replace a high value thing with a thing of even higher value to the dog. This way, if the dog is eating or chewing something it shouldn't be—like a slipper or something—their owners can easily take it back. Or if someone goes near the dog while it's eating a bone, the dog won't get aggressive.

I was a murderer of conversations.

It was like I was
walking on a tightrope.
If you take a wrong
step, you fall either to
your left or right. To
the left was speaking
too much. To the right
was speaking too little.
And my big clumsy feet
made it hard to keep
my balance.

I'd get up and try again, but still I kept falling
to the left, to the right, to the left . . . It always
ended up the same.

Ouch.

Landed right
on his face.

Ow . . .

Anyhoo . . .

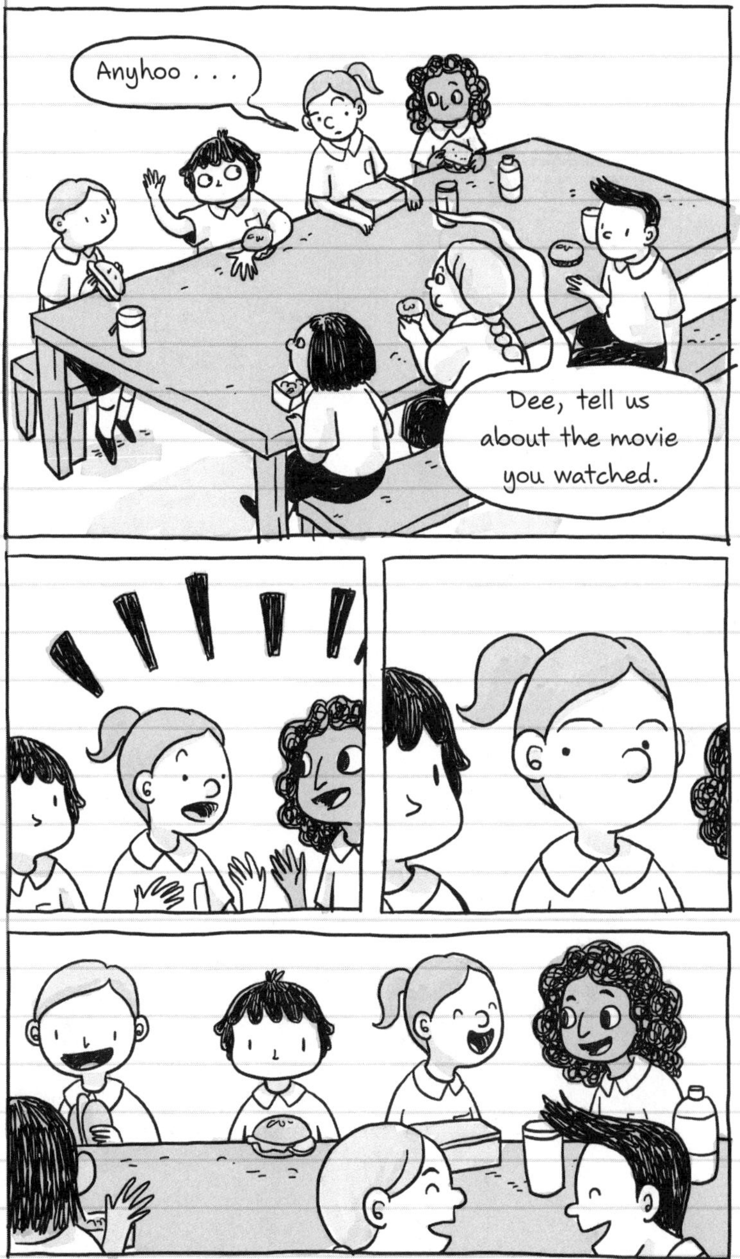
Anyhoo . . .
Dee, tell us about the movie you watched.

I can't say what Pheebs's look meant, since I can't read minds, but I know how it made me feel.

Despite my failures at tightrope walking, I didn't give up. I tried a different tactic—copying the other kids at the table.

First, I tried to be like Dee. Everyone likes Dee.

I tried to be like Pheebs.

And then I tried to be every one of everyone else.

I didn't always succeed in transforming into someone the other kids liked, but I could tell Pheebs was happier with me. She smiled more my way. But all those days, I'd get home from school and just curl up on my bed.

Popo, Mom, and Jie would ask if I was sick. They'd press their hands onto my forehead. They'd serve me cooling teas. *I'm fine, Mom.* They'd ask if I was being bullied at school. *I'm fine, Jie.* All I wanted was to be alone for a bit, but only weirdos like to be alone.

I guess Step 5 to Henry Khoo's Transformation into Fly on the Wall was my attempts at transforming into someone else. It led to Step 6.

## STEP 6 IN HENRY KHOO'S TRANSFORMATION INTO FLY ON THE WALL

Pheebs,
did you know?
It was shortly after the day
that Tim and I transformed

into weird poodles.
In the middle of March,
during lunch break,
Henry the poodle had gone to the bathroom.
Not a fire hydrant or a tree.
By the time he got to the table,
the magpies were already chirping away.
And Henry the poodle froze
with his lunch box in his paws.
No one noticed him there.
He didn't know who he should transform into,
what mask he should put on
that would make you happy.
And the truth is,
masks are heavy,
acting is tiring,
when you have to do it five days a week for months.
But no one likes the real Henry.
He's too talkative.
Too blunt.
Too quiet.
Too awkward.
But still Henry the poodle was so tired
he wanted to take a break.
Just forty-five minutes of sitting quietly
and just . . . being.

He felt like it was time for a WALK! NOW!

felt like a growl was about to explode into a WOOF!

felt like all his tightly wound curls were about to
SPROING!

His eyes, body, and legs turned.

He trotted away.

The lights in the airplane cabin are dimmed. I'm
glad Nor won't see the tears pooling in my eyes.

Then, in the midst of that darkness, there comes

a **SNAP!**

**SNAP!**

I blink, blink.
There's someone
standing next to
my row.

It's . . .

Gulp.

Just then, there's a jolt.

"No need to be afraid," Nor says. "It's just the plane's landing gear, a.k.a. wheels, being retracted into the plane. No need to be afraid. We're not doomed."

I am afraid. And I am doomed.

Instead of escaping the very person I'm fleeing from, I'm stuck up in the air with him.

Popo's deities sure have a devil-shaped funny bone.

I lean out of my seat, into the aisle. The attendant ushers Tim the Frog in the Well to the front of the plane. He hasn't seen me.

"Umm, Nor? Where is this plane going?" I ask, not sure I want to know the answer.

"Singapore. Why? Do you think you're on the wrong flight?"

"I was just testing you." Tim Aditya is supposed to be on his way to New York. Maybe he got on the wrong flight. But that can't be. His parents are flying with him. Adults don't make such silly mistakes.

When Tim the Frog reaches the curtain that separates Economy Class from Business Class, he turns his head. His eyes catch mine.

Tim disappears behind the curtain.

My nemesis is a Business Class passenger. And he means business.

Maybe Tim the Frog is a genius. He witnessed my crime back at school, but at the time, he knew he had no proof. He's been trying to find it, to take revenge for the comic I made about him and for not telling Principal Trang that I gifted that black eye to myself. Somehow, he then convinced his parents to get on this flight.

He's truly the evil mastermind in wuxia dramas, who stands around going . . .

**MUAHAHAHA**

The disciple in Popo's wuxia dramas faces obstacles, and overcoming each obstacle leads him to another, and another. That series of obstacles leads him to the place where he has to face the nemesis, beat him, and learn the ultimate wisdom.

There must be a reason why I ended up thousands of feet up in the air with my nemesis. I'm here to thwart Frog in the Well.

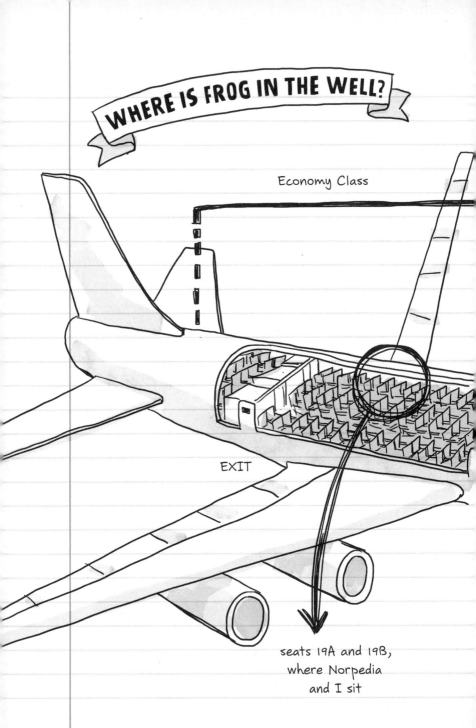

WHERE IS FROG IN THE WELL?

Economy Class

EXIT

seats 19A and 19B,
where Norpedia
and I sit

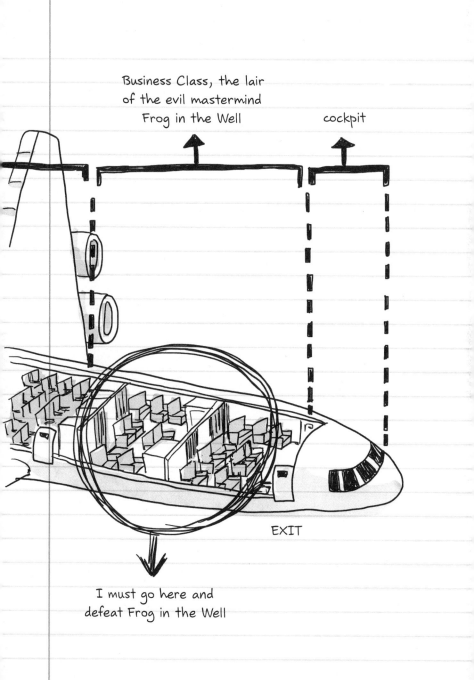

Business Class, the lair
of the evil mastermind
Frog in the Well

cockpit

EXIT

I must go here and
defeat Frog in the Well

To spy what the evil genius Frog is up to, I must go forth now.

What are you doing? Where are you going? The seat belt light is still on.

To spy on what the evil-but-genius Frog is up to, I must go forth as soon as the seat belt light is turned off.

Nor says, "Statistics say there's a higher chance of me being crushed by a meteor, getting injured by a toilet, or becoming a professional basketball player."

"A higher chance than what?" I ask.

She doesn't reply. That probably happens less often than getting injured by a toilet.

I look up from my notebook. She wasn't talking to me, after all.

"Nor?" I ask. "Are you afraid of—"

Her eyes shoot open. "Were you going to the bathroom?"

"That's private. And speaking from experience, the video games are really, really fun." I remove the console from her armrest and pick out the HI-YA! game for her. That will give her something to do besides death-gripping the armrests and butting into my business. "In this game, the character is a martial arts disciple. There's an evil mastermind who's terrorizing the town. So he bids his very old shifu—that's, like, his martial arts teacher—"

"I know what a shifu is. I have all the *HI-YA!* comics. I didn't know there's a game, though."

A FELLOW *HI-YA!* FAN! "My friend and I used to play this all the time at my house. You can name your disciple character and customize how you want them to look. Short or tall. Long hair, short hair. Hair color . . ."

Nor lets go of her armrests to grab the console. "Let me do it." She designs her character to be:

HI-YA!

. . .
What a great imagination.

Now, what does Henry the disciple have to do?

!!! How did you—
Oh, you're talking about the game.

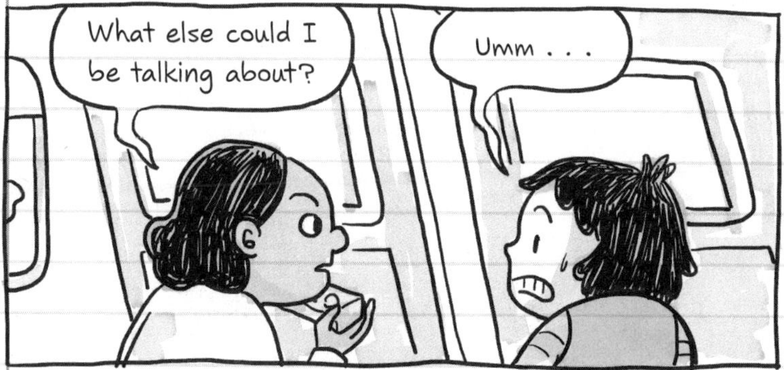
What else could I be talking about?
Umm . . .

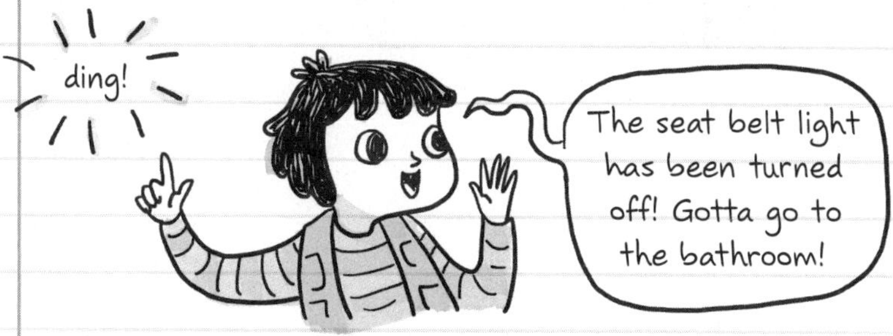
ding!
The seat belt light has been turned off! Gotta go to the bathroom!

Nor rolls her eyes. "How old do you think I am to fall for that? You're keeping secrets. First secret: You know someone named Frog in the Well. Second secret: You're some kind of disciple. Third secret: You aren't going to the bathroom."

"I'm going to Business Class, okay? It's like . . ." I point to her entertainment screen. "I'm like that Henry. I need to defeat the evil mastermind to restore peace. And the evil mastermind's name is Frog in the Well, and his lair is in Business Class."

"Ooooh." She clasps her hands together. "I can be your shifu."

"No way." I don't know if a twelve-year-old who's

afraid of flying can help take down someone as slimy as Frog in the Well.

"Why not?"

"You're younger than me." No point telling her that I guessed that she's afraid. I don't like people telling me I'm quiet or weird or a baby.

"Doesn't mean I'm not wiser."

She is wiser, for sure, about rules and being a know-it-all.

"For example," she says, "I know how to get you into Business Class."

"Who doesn't? Step one: Push the curtain aside. Step two: Walk in."

She shakes her head. "Tsk tsk tsk. How foolish you are, my little disciple. You can't just waltz into Business la-di-da. Otherwise, everyone would be paying for Economy tickets and sneaking into Business to enjoy the extra legroom and the cheese platter."

Right. Like I'm going to take advice from a kid younger than me. I march up to Business Class.

I'm sorry. Only Business Class passengers are permitted in there.

Darn, Nor's going to be all *I told you so, I told you so.*

"Where are your parents?" the attendant asks.

"Uh . . . they're at . . . home." That's the story of my life. When it really matters, I can't come up with a lie to save my butt.

"Who are you traveling with, then?"

"Uh . . . with . . . myself." Story. Of. My. Life.

The flight attendant's nose flares. She seems like the kind of adult who has forgotten what it's like to be a kid. "Nice try. Go back to your seat before I find your parents and tell them you're trying to sneak into Business Class."

"Huh? But they're really—"

"Please."

Sigh. I schlep back to my seat and suffer the greatest humiliation of my life.

Told.

You.

So.

I groan.

Popo taught me a Chinese idiom: 饥不择食, 寒不择衣, 慌不择路, which means "When you're hungry, you can't be choosy about food; when you're cold, you can't be choosy about clothes; when you're in a panic, you can't be choosy about which road to take." When I'm a lone wanderer desperate for wisdom, I can't be choosy about who my shifu is.

Shifu!

**COUNTDOWN TO TOUCHDOWN**

| 0 | 4 | | 3 | 9 |
|---|---|---|---|---|
| **HOURS** | | | **MINUTES** | |

Strapped into 19B

Now that I have a shifu, I'm no longer a lone wanderer. I transform into . . .

**THE DISCIPLE!**

 Shifu Nor keeps interrogating me about what's going on between me and the evil mastermind in Business Class, but I can't tell her that I'm Fly on the Wall who spreads gossip and rumors. She might tell everyone and comment on the blog that Henry Khoo is Fly on the Wall. Worse: She might hate me and not want to be my shifu.

 "Private," I keep telling her.

 "We're in a tin can high up in the air, and our fate is in the hands of a pilot we've never met! A pigeon could fly into the engine propeller! An alien spaceship could crash into our plane! And you're worried about privacy?"

I make a zipping-up motion across my lips.

"Fine! Fine!" she says, then dispenses some wisdom:

1. I have to sneak into Business Class at the right moment.
2. We have to wait for the right moment. An attendant is often near the curtain. Watch the gap below the curtain. Usually there's a pair of feet in black shoes there.
3. Do everything my shifu says.

She loosens her seat belt a tiny bit, just enough to allow her to peek over the seats. "Looks clear now. Go! Go! Go!"

But as I'm about to go, she pulls me back. "Abort! Feet under the curtains again!"

This happens a few more times. Once, I get as far as row 12 before the feet under the curtains reappear. I have no choice but to turn back toward 19B.

"Looks like the right moment is very fleeting," Shifu Nor says. "Are there any empty seats up front?"

I stand up and crane my neck. "There's an empty seat in the first row of Economy. Row 10. Oh! That's where the Official Ba—the kids from the Unaccompanied Minors Program are sitting."

"Sit there and wait for the right moment."

"What if they ask me what I'm doing sitting there?"

"Tell them the person sitting next to you has bad breath. That is an outrageous lie, but I'm willing to make sacrifices for the success of your mission."

I don't tell her what I'm really afraid of—that when the Official Babies talk to me, what happened with the chatty magpies might happen all over again.

A week after I stopped sitting at that table, I was feeling more relaxed, more like myself. But I was also lonely. Yes, yes, yes. It was my own fault. No one kicked me off that table, and I'm pretty sure they'd have welcomed me back if I wanted to return.

Not long after I got lonely, I spotted Pheebs and Dee walking ahead of me in the hallway. I sped up. I thought I'd just say hi like nothing had happened and sit at that table again. Then I heard Pheebs.

Henry's family hovers over him so much he's like a helipad.

My sworn sister used my own joke against me. She had snorted juice when I told her that helipad joke about my family. I assumed then that she was laughing with me—turned out, she was laughing *at* me.

Then I heard Pheebs say something else.

Her words were daggers. They flew behind me, stabbed, and pierced right through to the other side.

She thought I was nothing but a misshapen turnip most people would just throw away. How long had she thought this? A week? A month? Forever and a day?

I didn't know my sworn sister hated me, looked down on me. I had gotten it so, so wrong. There must be a barometer inside each of us that measures how much another person likes or dislikes us. A friend-o-meter. Mine is broken. How do I know the next person who I think is a friend won't actually think I'm a pathetic joke? How do I know the next friend I make won't soon realize that I'm The Odd Bunch and toss me aside?

I guess finding out my friend-o-meter is broken was Step 7 of Henry Khoo's Transformation into Fly on the Wall.

Hesitating at 19B

I wish I could be cool and not care about what other people think of me. But I'm so not cool you could . . .

The thought of the Official Babies not liking me transforms my starchy vest into one made of porcupine quills poking me all over. My skinny jeans turn into Saran wrap squeezing my legs. My boots fill up with scorching sand burning my feet.

"I'd come with you to make sure you don't screw up," Nor says, "but I promised to call my parents once I'm in the air." She takes out a credit card and inputs the numbers into the entertainment screen to purchase in-flight Wi-Fi. "My dad loaned me his card."

"He loaned you his card? What if you buy a million toys? A hovercraft?"

She laughs. "He trusts me."

Life is so unfair. Okay, yes, I'm much, much luckier than many kids, but Nor is luckier than I am. Her family trusts her with responsibilities. Not "responsibilities" like taking out the trash. Real ones where you have power and the potential to abuse it, like Spider-Man's.

But Nor calling her parents reminds me I have to purchase Wi-Fi so my family can text and call me while I'm in the air. Through the entertainment screen, I buy 500 MB of data, using Mom's credit card numbers that I already memorized. I make a mental note to return $25.70 to Mom later.

Once I'm connected, my phone beeps with two messages, both sent about ten minutes ago.

jie called. Told her u're out in the backyard in the cubbyhouse with the rest of the ppl working on our group project. They all made extra noises so ur sis would think ure having too much fun 2 come 2 the phone. Maomi didn't want to bark, so Dee barked.

I had no idea Pheebs had friends over at her place. The only reason I told my family I'm doing a project with Pheebs and six other classmates was because I knew they wouldn't say no to an opportunity for me to make more friends. As long as it didn't involve falling from a height or infectious diseases or extreme weather or very sharp things—all threats on this plane except for the last one. But I made it all up.

Did Pheebs get the idea for this gathering from my alibi? Or had she planned it even before I came up with The Plan?

And did her plan include not inviting me?

195

I also have no idea how she even got those kids to agree to come over. When Fly on the Wall outed Pheebs as a backstabber in "Wolf Stalks Chatswood School" six weeks ago, the magpies at that table started looking at her differently, like they had an eye disease and could only squint at her in suspicion. It hadn't been my goal, but I thought maybe she'd leave the table and hang out with me again. I know, I know—I'm selfish.

"It's all good, Dad," Nor says into her phone, jolting me out of my thoughts and back to the greatest adventure everrr.

I quickly reply to Jie before she calls the police on me for being a second late in responding to her text.

Don't call me. I'm very busy. I'll text. And I'm fine. First aid kit not needed at all.

"Dad, Dad! I'm a shifu now—" Nor cups a hand over her phone and whispers to me, "What are you still doing here? Go!"

I go. I'm going to try harder at making friends so that Step 6 of Henry Khoo's Transformation into Fly on the Wall—walking away from potential friends—

doesn't happen again. I don't know who I should transform into. Or have I transformed already?

Vinai then goes back to playing a game on his entertainment unit. All the other kids are playing games, too.

I look at Vinai's screen. "Oh, it's *HI-YA!* I used to play this game a lot too."

"Cool." Vinai's disciple character eats a magic flower and transforms into a dinosaur. It's trying to get out of a room, but the door won't open.

I watch the pair of feet under the curtain separating me from Business Class and get ready to slip behind it. Any moment now.

"Have you defeated the evil mastermind?" Vinai asks.

"I have to get to Business Class first."

He yanks off his earphones and turns to face me. "Huh?"

Uh-oh. I was so busy watching for the right timing to sneak into Business Class that I didn't think before I replied to Vinai. "Um . . . I mean . . ."

The other Official Babies turn to watch us.

"You see . . . I have a nemesis. He's like the villain mastermind in *HI-YA!* And he's sitting in Business Class. I'm like the disciple who has to get into the evil mastermind's lair and defeat him."

Vinai asks, "What's the evil mastermind's name?"

"Frog in the Well."

"That's not scary at all," the boy at 10A says.

"He may look harmless, but believe me, he is a poisonous type of frog," I say. "If I don't sneak into Business Class and defeat him, I'll be treated like a baby forever."

The kids sitting farther away from me have to wait until the information is passed down the conga line to them. When they do, each and every one of them nods. They get what it's like to be treated like you can't do anything yourself.

"What's going on here?" the Official Babysitter,

who is seated at the other end of row 10, looks up from her book and asks.

Before I can tell the kids not to tell the Babysitter the truth, the kid next to her points at me.

That disciple is about to defeat the evil mastermind Frog in the Well.

"You kids . . ." The Official Babysitter furrows her eyebrows. "Have such wild imaginations." She goes back to reading her book, and the rest of us grin at one another. Sometimes, telling an adult the truth is the surest way to make them not take you seriously.

"Excuse me," another adult voice says. I turn to see a flight attendant with a food trolley in the aisle next to me. "Would you like seafood pasta or chicken with rice?" he asks.

"Umm . . . This isn't my seat. I'd better get back." I get up, but the trolley is blocking my way out of the row.

"Why don't you eat here?" Vinai says. "It doesn't

matter where you sit, you know. I mean, as long as the seat's not taken."

THESE KIDS ACTUALLY WANT TO HANG OUT WITH ME, HENRY KHOO!

Cool.

"And as long as you're not an Economy passenger sitting in Business," Vinai adds, wriggling his eyebrows up and down.

HE'S SHARING AN INSIDE JOKE WITH ME, HENRY KHOO!

Cool.

"What's your name, Disciple?" Anita asks.

"Disciple Fly on the Wall."

"Fly and Frog! Great names for enemies!"

Everyone nods and laughs. With me. I'm no longer the scientist observing from the outside.

I adjust my tiny party hat and clear my throat. "I need your help to defeat the Frog."

COUNTDOWN TO TOUCHDOWN

0 3 : 2 5
HOURS MINUTES

Hanging out with the Official Babies at row 10

Over lunch, the Official Babies cook up a few schemes for defeating Frog in the Well.

I say we flush Frog in the Well out with a reward.

WANTED

$1,000 REWARD

Rat Vinai

I only have $236.90.

Let's just croak loudly until Frog in the Well leaves his lair.

RIBBIT RIBBIT RIBBIT RIBBIT

Rat Anita

How about we get a trench coat? Henry can sit on my shoulders.
Rat Evelyn
And we'll have to track down a gold watch and a hat to wear. We'll look like a rich adult and we can just walk into Business Class.

Maybe we clog the toilet at the back . . .
Rat Chingyuan
. . . and all the attendants will be busy unclogging the toilet, and Henry can sneak into Business.
Rat Chingtan

This is the second time I've ever hung out with a big group of kids. I'm feeling a little rusty talking to everyone, since I'm inexperienced, but I don't feel uncomfortable like I did with the magpies. I can actually imagine myself being friends with the Official Babies. It's as if I'm only now realizing there are other people in this world. I mean, I knew other people existed, but it was like Pheebs wore a miner's helmet.

I got lost in her glare and couldn't see anything else. Now that she has turned away from me and I've stopped chasing her, I can see the other potential friends that have always been there.

Yet I can't help missing Pheebs.

Feelings are like vegetables. You don't like them, but they're always piled on your plate anyway.

After I overheard Pheebs calling me a helipad and The Odd Bunch, it felt like I was a stowaway on a pirate ship and I'd been discovered.

I floated aimlessly around the school. No one paid any attention to me.

I floated
farther
and farther
to the zone of the flotsam.

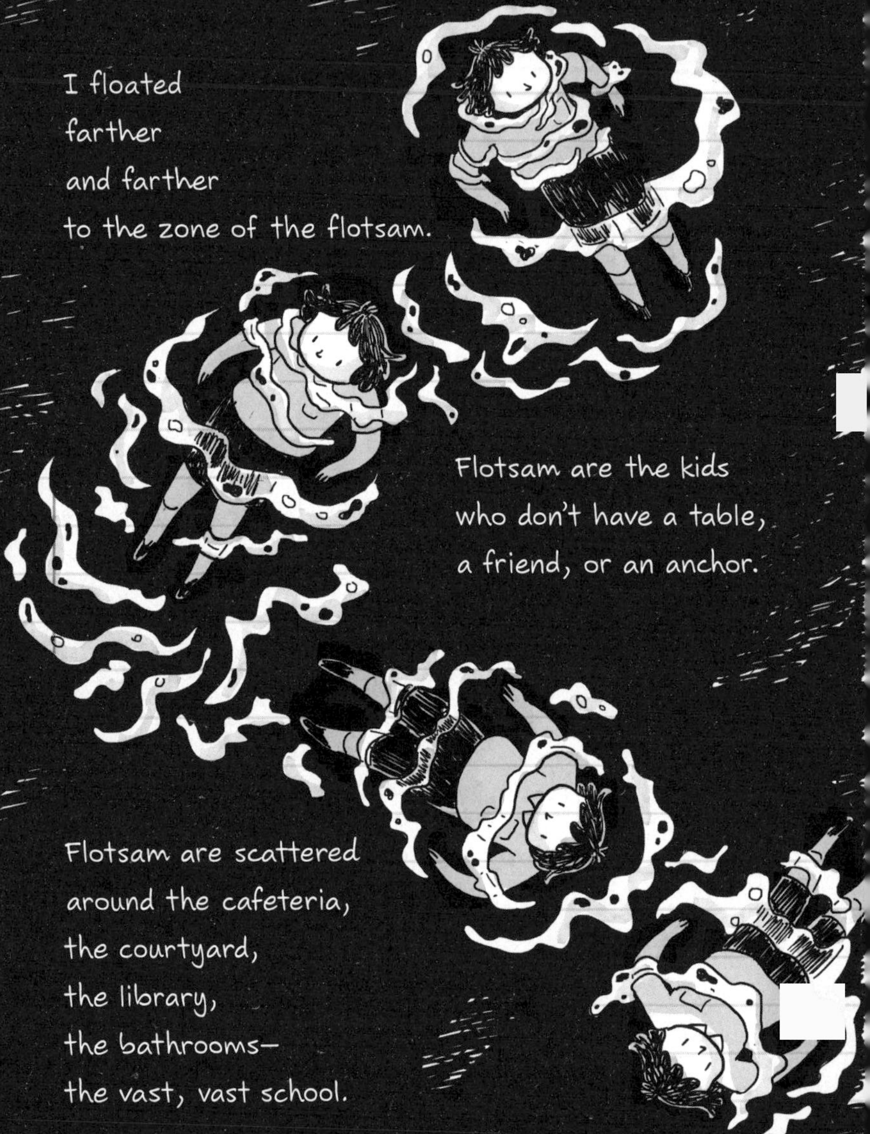

Flotsam are the kids
who don't have a table,
a friend, or an anchor.

Flotsam are scattered
around the cafeteria,
the courtyard,
the library,
the bathrooms—
the vast, vast school.

Floating about sounds relaxing
like watching cartoons
while munching on chips,

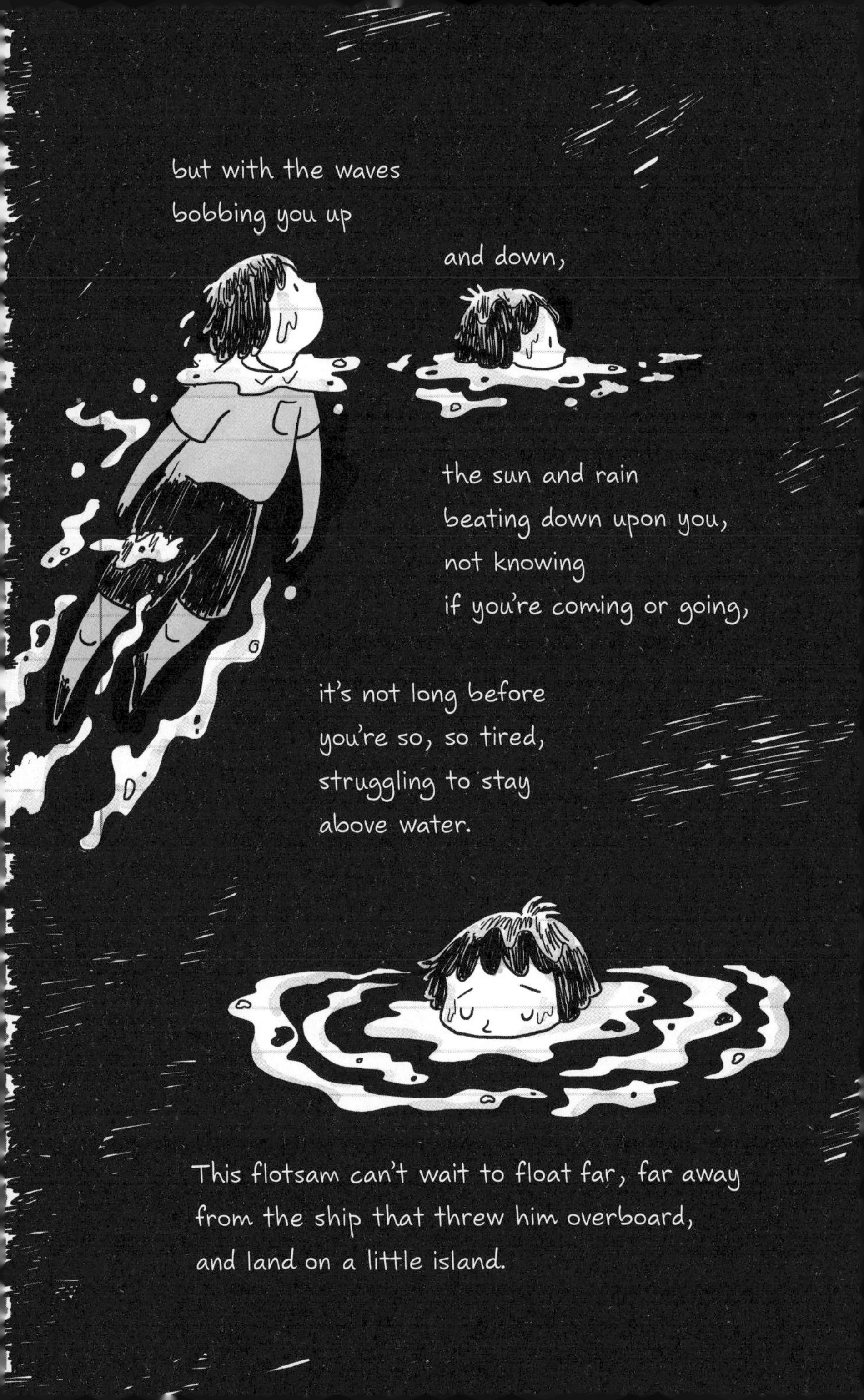
but with the waves
bobbing you up
and down,
the sun and rain
beating down upon you,
not knowing
if you're coming or going,
it's not long before
you're so, so tired,
struggling to stay
above water.
This flotsam can't wait to float far, far away
from the ship that threw him overboard,
and land on a little island.

Back then, as I floated aimlessly, no one paid any attention to me.

I was like a Fly on the Wall.

roadkill

So in late March, this fly buzzed into the computer laboratory by himself. Just to occupy its loneliness, it picked up a tablet and stylus. They were like the ones used in Digital Art for Kids. The fly drew a digital comic, using the things it had seen and heard around school for inspiration. Making the comics gave it a chance to test out the new skills it had recently learned.

And then it posted the comic online, naming itself and the blog *Fly on the Wall*.

Henry Khoo's Transformation into Fly on the Wall was complete.

"Disciple Fly," Vinai says, snapping me out of my thoughts, "you look constipated. Did you think up a good idea?"

"I—"

BZZ!

Vinai looks around. "Is there a fly?"

"It's my phone vibrating in my pocket—" Hold on . . . Fly! That's the key to getting into Business Class! "I have a stupendous scheme!"

I tell the Official Babies all about the Stupendous Scheme. It involves me transforming into an insignificant fly, just like back in school, during the final step of my Transformation into Fly on the Wall.

The flight attendants are like professional bug swatters. They're much more observant than the people at school. If a fly tries to buzz into Business Class, they will notice it. And squash it.

I need a distraction. That's where the Official Babies come in. They need to turn into bugs that are even more hated than flies. There's a bug that makes Jie drop everything and arm herself with bug spray. The Official Babies will turn into . . .

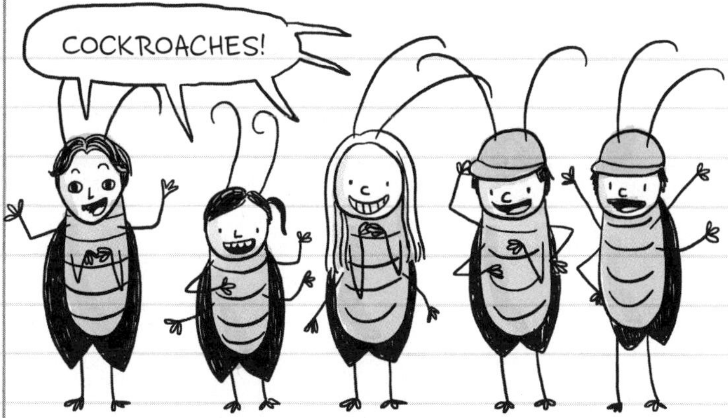
COCKROACHES!

**THE STUPENDOUS SCHEME BEGINS!**

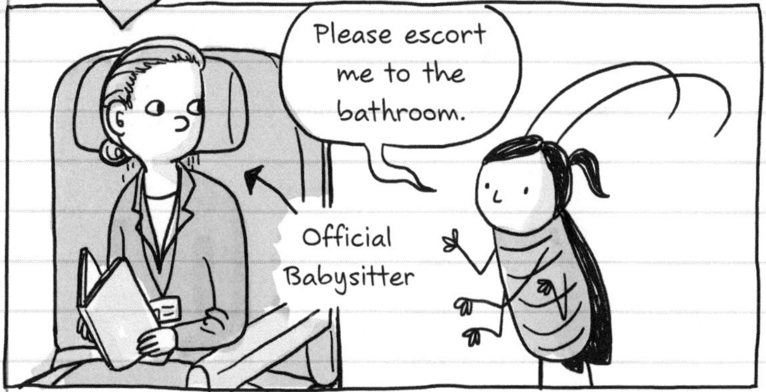
Please escort me to the bathroom.
Official Babysitter

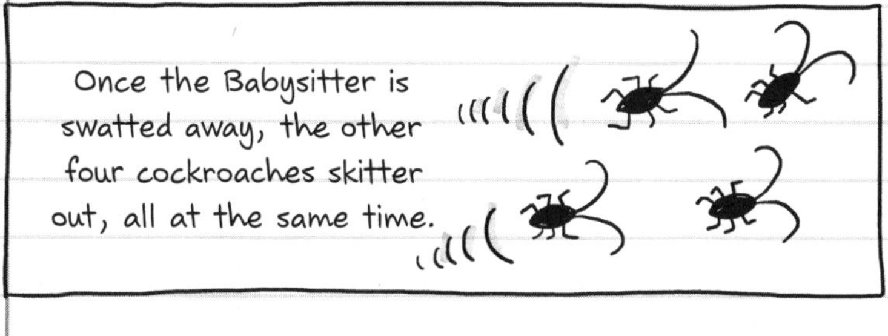
Once the Babysitter is swatted away, the other four cockroaches skitter out, all at the same time.

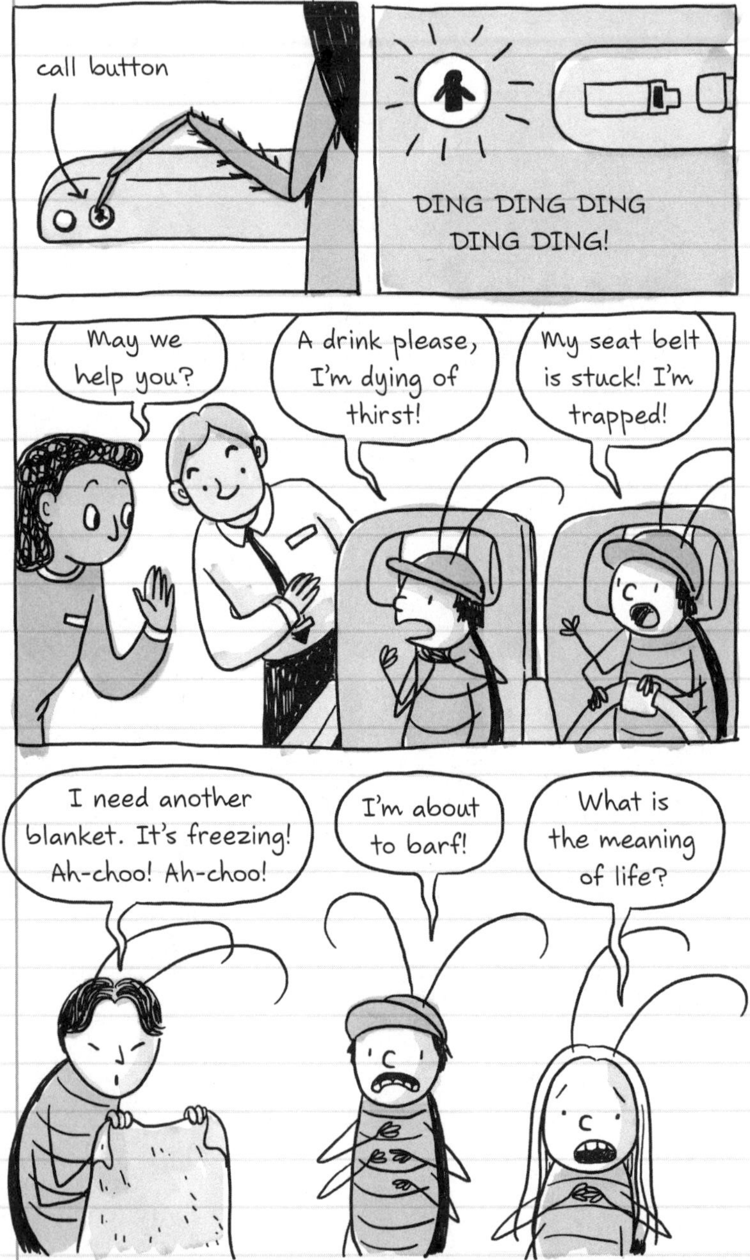
call button
DING DING DING DING DING!
May we help you?
A drink please, I'm dying of thirst!
My seat belt is stuck! I'm trapped!
I need another blanket. It's freezing! Ah-choo! Ah-choo!
I'm about to barf!
What is the meaning of life?

The Fly is now inside Business Class, ready for serious business.

I fly undetected into an empty seat. Except it isn't empty. The tray table is open, and there's food on it. The passenger must be in the bathroom or something.

As I'm scanning the horizon for the Frog's head, a flight attendant approaches. Luckily he's smiling, and he isn't the one who stopped me from entering earlier. "What's your name, sir?"

"Sir Fly—I mean—" Calm down, Henry Khoo. Remember what Shifu Nor taught you to say if you're caught trespassing. "My—My name is Tim Aditya. I was just walking around, stretching my legs."

The attendant fishes out a piece of paper from his pocket. I peek. It's a list of names, and Tim Aditya is on it. "Well, Mr. Aditya, we've just served the special-requirements meal. Lunch for the rest of the passengers will be served shortly." The attendant walks away, and that's when I spot the Frog in the Well.

Only the top of his head, with the coarse broom-like hair, sticks out above his seat, like a nemesis from a wuxia drama lying in ambush. His parents are seated in the row in front of him, enjoying their cheese platters, unaware of their son's evil deeds.

I buzz over, my wings beating faster and faster. He might leap up at any time.

But he doesn't.

His attention is on his phone. I hear the SNAP! SNAP! SNAP! of his camera shutter. I buzz closer.

FROG!

What's up?

Before I can tell Tim to stop smirking, someone else shouts, "This is outrageous!"

There's now a woman at that seat I perched on a minute ago. Her face is lobster-red, and her mouth is an upside down U. She's pressing the call button repeatedly. The call button light goes on and off with DING! DING! DING! noises. The attendant who thinks I'm Tim Aditya attends to her.

You served me cashews? And half-eaten ones?

MIXED NUTS

The attendant takes the packet. "I'm so sorry! This bag of mixed nuts is not part of our meal. I don't know how an Economy Class snack got here."

The half-eaten packet of mixed nuts that I stuffed in my vest after it almost killed me is . . .

pat
pat
pat

. . . gone.

It must have fallen out.
I look up.

I almost killed someone.

COUNTDOWN TO TOUCHDOWN

| O | 2 | 5 | O |

**HOURS    MINUTES**

Fleeing back to Economy Class

It's Game Over.

"Disciple Fly? Did you defeat the evil mastermind?" Vinai calls out, but I continue wobbling down the aisle.

Before I even sit down, Nor asks, "Did you take down Frog in the Well? Was it sweet victory?"

"I . . ." I can't tell her I almost killed someone. "I need to check my phone. I got a message earlier."

**JIE**
**WETALK**

The first aid kit is also for others around you who might get hurt.

Jie sent this message about twenty minutes ago. How could she have predicted that I would almost kill someone?

I reply to her.

What?

That accident with the bicycle . . . the cars around you . . .
Back then, at Pheebs's birthday . . .

You're lucky the cars didn't hit you, or each other or anything or anyone else.
I never even thought about that . . .
And that other accident with Tim Aditya.
I was the one who got hurt. My black eye.
Principal Trang told Mom about what happened AFTER Tim punched you and gave you that black eye . . . The janitor's cart . . . After you bumped into it . . .
WHUMP!

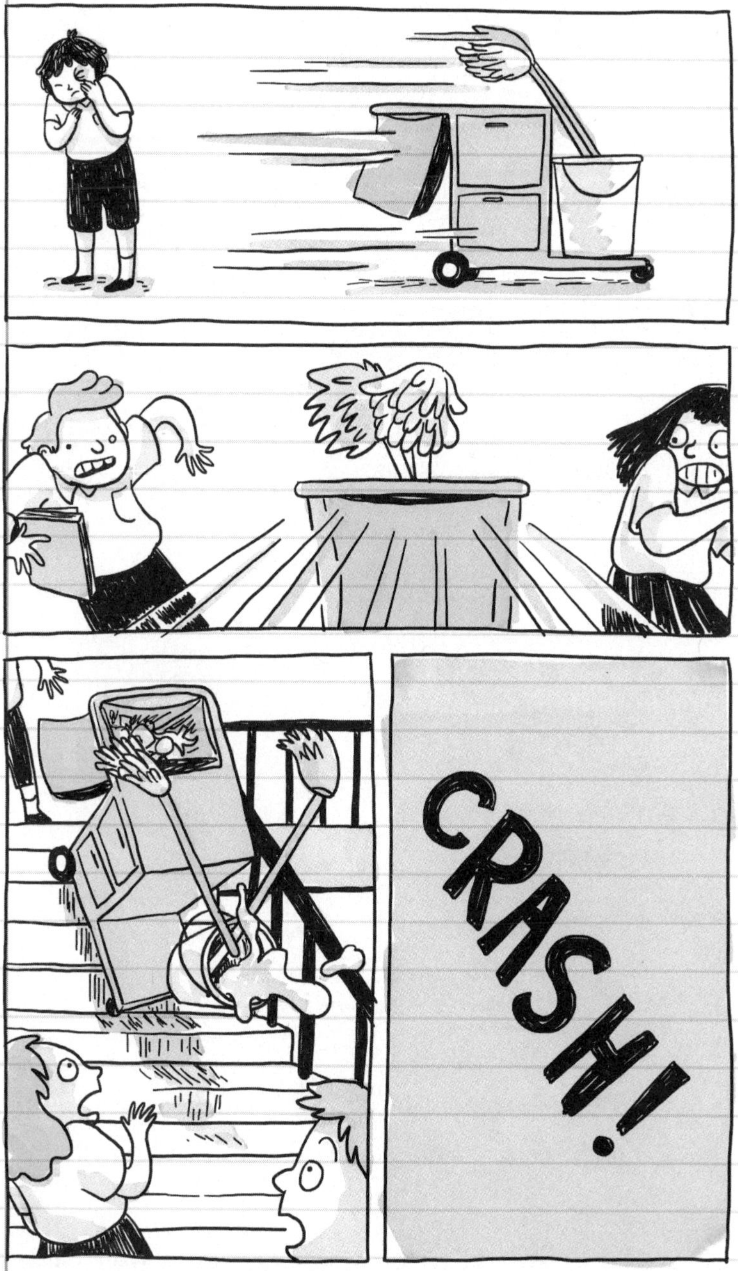
CRASH!

It could have been a disaster.

I never thought about that cart either.

That's just it.
I wasn't thinking.
And I definitely wasn't thinking when I posted that comic about the lovebirds.

# FLY ON THE WALL

## HOW TO TELL IF SOMEONE LIKES SOMEBODY

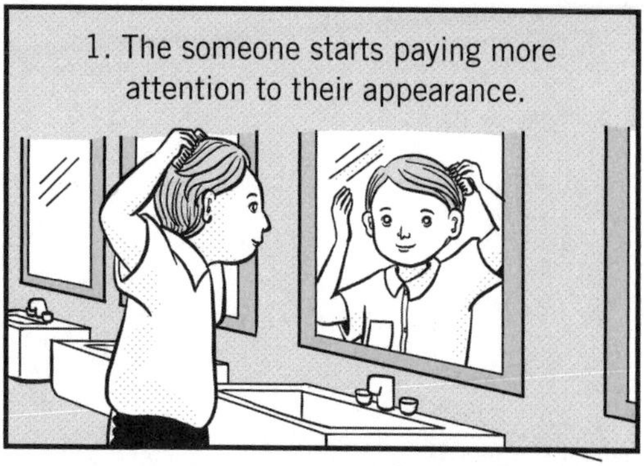
1. The someone starts paying more attention to their appearance.

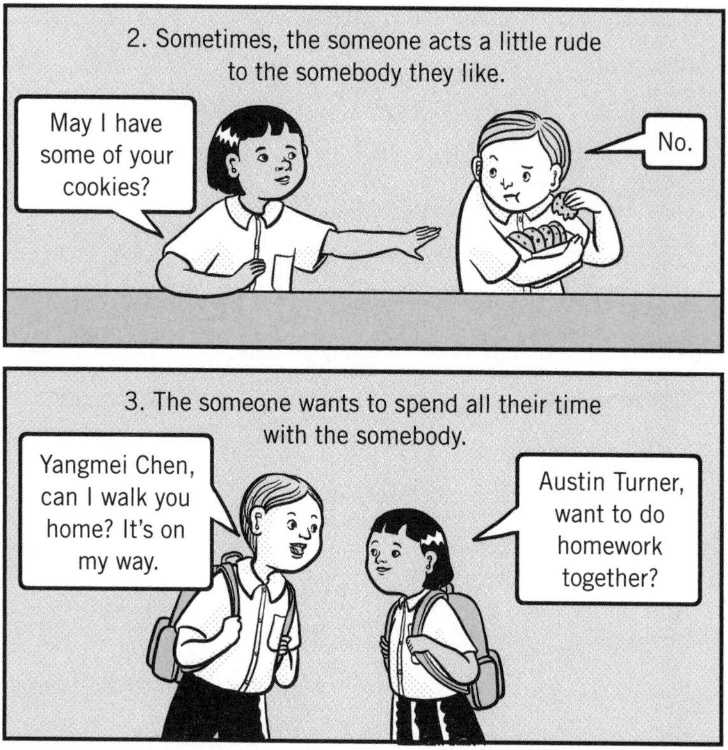
2. Sometimes, the someone acts a little rude to the somebody they like.
May I have some of your cookies?
No.
3. The someone wants to spend all their time with the somebody.
Yangmei Chen, can I walk you home? It's on my way.
Austin Turner, want to do homework together?

After that post was published, the other students made smooching noises every time Austin and Yangmei were in the same room. They started avoiding each other. At that table with the magpies, they'd sit at opposite ends. I ruined their happily ever after.

"Disciple Fly." Nor's voice jolts me back to my adventure. The adventure where I almost killed someone. "Tell Shifu Nor what happened!"

"The disciple failed. That's all." I lean away from her, against the armrest by the aisle. Since my fingernails have been chewed bloody, I concentrate on deciding which parts of my finger I could still chew without officially turning into a cannibal. That distracts me from thoughts that might make me cry.

Nor loosens her seat belt a little so she can turn and grab my hands. "Stop eating your hands—Oh, you stink!"

"What?"

She's pinching her nose. "B.O."

I deserve that, after what I did to Trevor Bannen in *Fly on the Wall*, Issue #7.

# FLY ON THE WALL

SKUNK SPRAYS CHATSWOOD SCHOOL

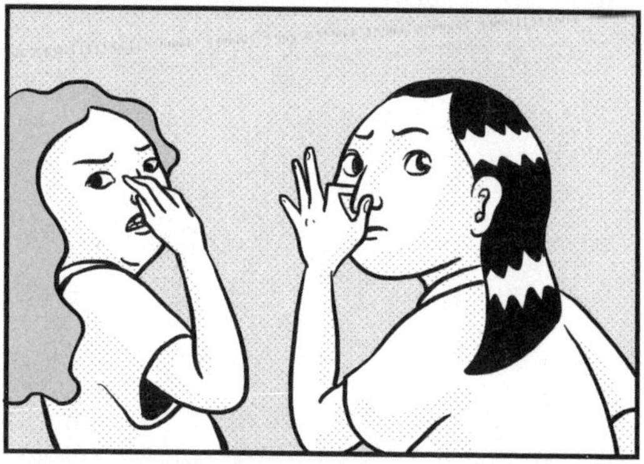

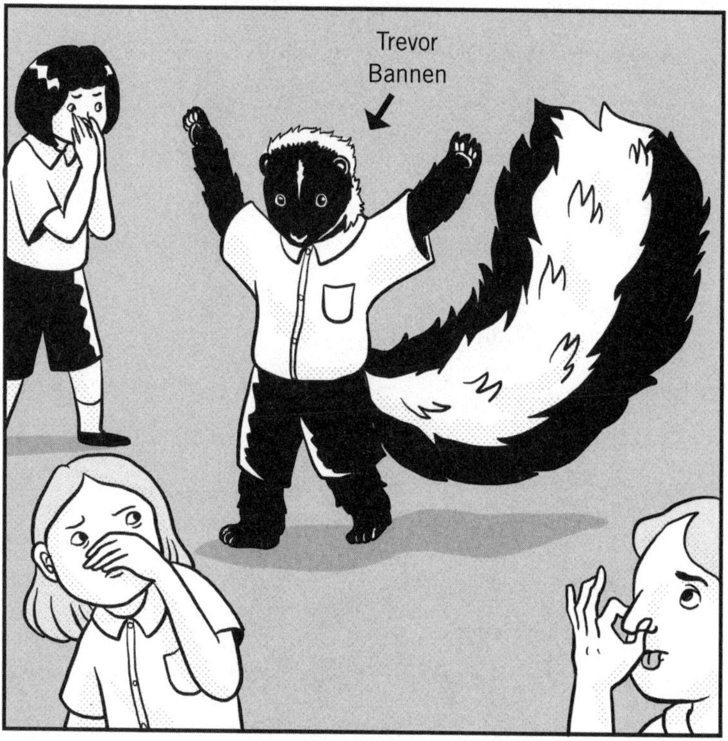
Trevor Bannen

I'd simply overheard two sixth graders in the gym talk about how Trevor Bannen has body odor. I don't actually know who he is. But I do know that "Skunk Sprays Chatswood School" got the second highest number of comments at 367.

Now, for the first time, I think about Trevor Bannen— what he looks like, if he's the kind of kid who'd laugh about the comic, or if he'd get upset like I would have.

I keep picturing the face of the woman I almost killed, except her body is on that of a boy in a Chatswood School uniform. I hurt Trevor Bannen like I almost hurt that woman. Really badly.

Someone once commented on Fly on the Wall:

💬 **Comments** (322)                    **Comment**

**Newest**          Oldest

**SuperPete**, 2 months ago
Fly, you're a virus.
                              Replies (3) | Reply

All along, I assumed they meant my blog had gone viral. But the truth is . . .

I am a virus. I hurt people.

## TO EVERYONE AT CHATSWOOD

I hadn't planned to hurt you.
I was filling up the loneliness of recess and lunch break.
I'd been feeling like
the fancy plate Mom never used, locked in the cabinet
the dress Jie never wore, the tag still hanging
the long sentences Dad never said to me, their
meanings unknown
the guitar never strummed, its strings silent
the car never driven
the can never opened
the book never read.

If Henry Khoo disappeared,
you wouldn't have noticed.
No one in Chatswood would have noticed.
But Fly on the Wall was on everyone's lips and minds.
When the blog went viral,
the comments that poured in
were like Halloween night candy.
I was so hopped up on sugar
that even though I knew the comics would hurt you,
I didn't think about how much.
I continued
because those comments,

even if they were from strangers,
even if some were angry faces, not love hearts,
they were the only evidence
that I exist.
And I want to exist.

I didn't realize
how much force is in each step I take
until I stubbed my toe.

I just want a minute to think, but Nor isn't giving me one second. "I didn't get to spy on the Frog," I reply.

"What happened?"

"Nothing. I just didn't get a chance."

"You're lying. Why are you keeping secrets from your shifu?"

She's not really my shifu. A true shifu wouldn't have a fear of flying, or a fear of anything.

"Disciple Henry! Tell me!"

I smack my hands down on my armrests. "Are you a businessman?"

"If you're not a businessman," I say. "Then why are you all up in my business? You're not really my shifu, you know!"

Maybe the reason Pheebs needs friends other than me is not because my family hovers over me. Maybe the reason Dad doesn't like me is not because Popo, Mom, and Jie baby me.

The reason is me.

When Mom bought a nonstick pan that turned out to be sticky, she went back to the store for a refund. When Jie is angry with Maomi, she threatens to send him to the pound or back to his breeders. When the disciple in Popo's wuxia dramas causes big trouble, his shifu kicks him out.

Now Nor doesn't want me sitting next to her.

But . . .

. . . where do I go?

Back in 19B

I decided to seek shelter in the bathroom, but when I return to my seat, the end of the world—my world—strikes.

MY SECRET MANUAL IS GONE!

Popo taught me this idiom: 祸不单行, which means "misfortunes don't come in singles." Once again, Chinese idioms and proverbs and the old men in history who came up with them prove to be wisdomous. This is misfortune number three—first I offended my (fake) shifu, then, during my bathroom trip, misfortune number two happened.

I was washing my armpits to spare Nor my stink. It was the least I could do. Besides, there had been a very real danger that I might cry in front of her.

With nowhere else to go, I hid in the only private place on the plane—the bathroom.

In that tiny space, I took off my vest and my shirt. I reached my left arm over my head and leaned down to bring my stinky left armpit, with my first underarm hair, closer to the sink. That was when my lonely underarm hair took flight.

It fluttered

fluttered

fluttered

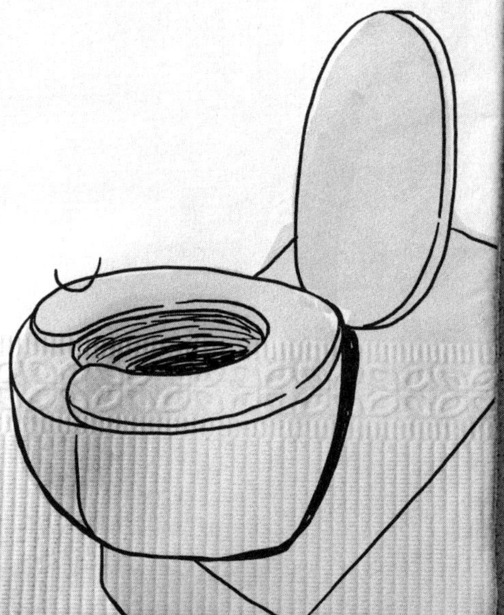

I studied the hair. I don't know how I could've mistaken a strand of Maomi's brown fur for my underarm hair. I guess I wanted my first underarm hair that badly. I guess I thought being a grown-up would fix everything. I guess I wanted to have something to ask Dad about. Something that might make him respond with multiple long sentences.

I blew a gentle puff. The hair fluttered into the bowl. I pressed flush. A loud whooshing echoed all around the bathroom as everything was sucked away.

It was over an hour later when someone knocked on the door. "Are you all right? You've been in the bathroom an awfully long time."

"I'm fine," I said.

"Do you need help?"

"No—No, I'm coming out."

When I reached 19B, I found one thing on it. My pen. Only my pen.

My book of secrets was gone.

"What did this kid look like?" I ask. "What did they say? Why didn't you stop them?"

Nor's video game character has turned into a unicorn and is stuck in the same room that Vinai's character got held up in, unable to open the door. "How would I know? I'm not a *businessman*."

It's such a good comeback I can't even be angry at her. But she's still angry at me. She turns back to her game.

There is only one person on this plane who knows me and might want my secret manual. A person who earlier crossed into the Economy section, where he doesn't belong. That person is none other than the evil mastermind, Tim Aditya, the Frog in the Well.

He must have taken that photo earlier to spy on the layout of the Economy section, and then quickly snuck in later on and stolen my secret manual. While I want to HI-YA! him, I must admit his stealth ninja skills are indeed A+.

He probably didn't have proof of my secret identity before, but he sure does now. He will hand the secret manual over to the grown-ups. Then I'll be Fly in Deep Doo-doo.

Knowing you're doomed is horrifying. But turns out, there are worse things. Like knowing you caused your own doom. By writing that manual, I was the one who gift wrapped and handed that proof to him.

Waitaminute! There's something even more horrifying!

Tim is not going to simply hand my secret manual to Principal Trang. Tim has been taking photos on his phone. He's probably taking photos of my secret manual right this second. He'll upload them online. He'll show the world my celebration of my first underarm hair. Or how I'm moping around just because my sworn sister found better friends. Or that I'm being selfish, being too sensitive, being too quiet, too everything.

My secret manual is supposed to only be discovered after I'm long dead. Because I can't be embarrassed then.

I can't blush.

Everyone finding out you're a gossiper stinks. But turns out, there are worse things.

Like everyone getting confirmation that you really are very, very weird.

**WHAT WILL HAPPEN WHEN PHOTOS OF MY SECRET MANUAL ARE PUBLISHED**

Henry Khoo . . .

. . . needs deodorant. He stinks!

He's obsessed with underarm hair. How weird!

He gets upset if you make a harmless comment about him. He's too sensitive!

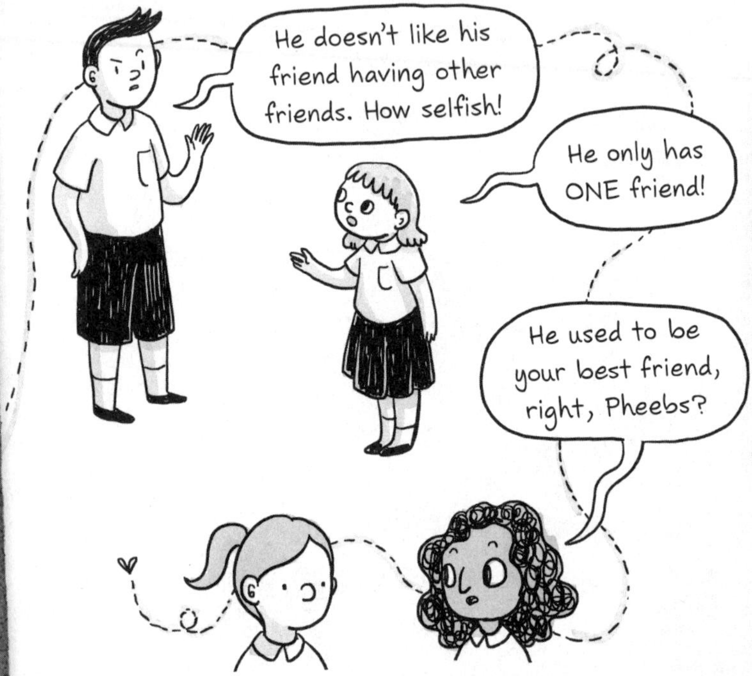
He doesn't like his friend having other friends. How selfish!
He only has ONE friend!
He used to be your best friend, right, Pheebs?

What would Pheebs say?

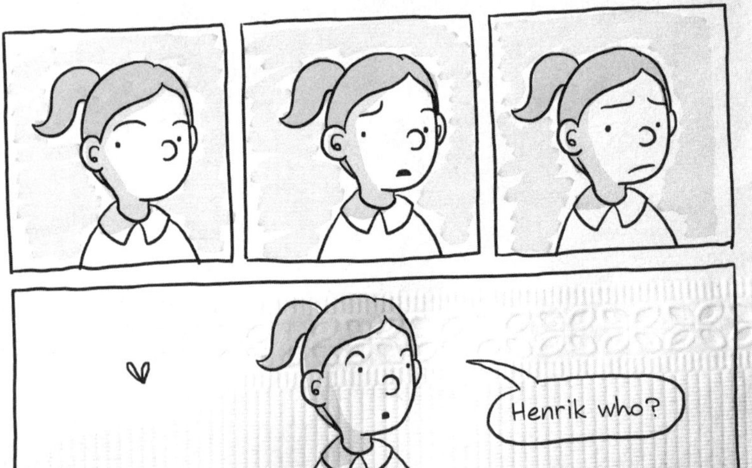
Henrik who?

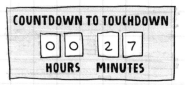

I used cash and bought a new notebook from the in-flight shop

The problem with the world is it doesn't stop just because a twelve-year-old declares that his life is over.

As I lie dying in my seat, the sun keeps on shining. The plane's wing continues slicing through the clouds. The attendants continue handing out orange juice.

"Yes!" Nor says. Her Henry character has transformed into an elephant, and it receives a messenger pigeon from his shifu. I can't see what the message is.

I miss Popo. I miss her ridiculous sayings that don't help solve my problems but make me laugh.

I call her.

 婆婆，武侠剧看的怎么样了？官府还在找那个徒弟吗？(Popo, how's your wuxia drama? Is the magistrate still hunting the disciple?)

 官府当然还在找，不过徒弟已经跑很远很远。(The magistrate is still hunting, but the disciple has run far, far away.)

 那个徒弟有没有想过放弃？(Does the disciple ever think of giving up?)

好几次。他的路不容易走。(A number of times. His journey isn't easy.)

 他的师父帮他解决问题就好了。(If only his shifu could solve his problems for him.)

 师父领进门，进步靠个人。(A teacher can open the door, but the disciple has to walk through it on his own.)

 太难了。那秘笈呢？秘笈在哪儿？(That's too hard. What about the secret manual? What happened to it?)

 你猜吧。你陪我看了那么多武侠剧。(Guess. You've watched enough wuxia dramas with me.)

 被大坏人偷了。那个徒弟怎样才能拿回秘笈呢？ (It got stolen by the evil mastermind. How can the disciple get it back?)

 他必须面对大坏人。(He has to confront the evil mastermind.)

 嗨。。。(Sigh . . .)

 师父说："千里之行始于足下。"那比"坐以待毙"好多。明白吗？(Shifu says, "A thousand-mile journey starts with one footstep." That's better than "sitting around waiting for the end." Do you understand?)

 明白。婆婆，我要做作业了。(Understood. Popo, I better get back to my project.)

I hang up.

But I don't know the first step I should take to solve my problem with the Frog. Maybe Nor will have ideas. "Nor . . ."

On her screen, elephant Henry eats a mushroom. It POOF!s into a sheep. Nor punches the buttons on her console, making sheep Henry run into the door over and over again.

I can't have Nor hating me like Pheebs will hate me when she finds out that I'm Fly. Even though Nor said mean things to me, I said mean things to her first. And she did help me get into Business Class.

But before I can apologize, Nor says, without looking at me, "Can I talk now?"

"Of course, I—"

"Sorry. I shouldn't have said what I said earlier. That was really mean."

"I'm—"

"I'm still not talking to you, though."

"Oh!" That's . . . new. I've never met a kid as straightforward as Nor. But then again I haven't gotten to know many kids at all. And it kills me to admit this:

Nor is more mature than I am. She's angry at me, yet she still can apologize for what she did wrong.

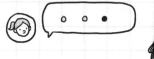 

What is Pheebs typing? Has Tim uploaded photos of my secret manual online?

Is Pheebs typing "I HATE U I HATE U I HATE U I HATE U I HATE U I HATE U I HATE U"?

The others wanted 2 walk Maomi so we took him 4 a walk thru the shopping strip. The one u and I used 2 go 2 with my dad. We were walking past that donut café when Maomi suddenly broke free and made a beeline toward some dude sitting on the couch inside. I was like ??? since Maomi doesn't give a 💩 about strangers. Then Maomi squeezed himself right between the dude and the person holding hands with the dude.

Phew. It's just Maomi and his cute, weird self.

245

Immediately, I open WeTalk and make a call. "Jie? Don't—"

A robotic voice interrupts me: "Your call has been disconnected. Please check your internet connection."

COUNTDOWN TO TOUCHDOWN

0 0 1 7

HOURS   MINUTES

HENRY KHOO
Got his wish for
an adventure . . .
in the underworld.

Jie will call Mom. Together, they will drive over the speed limit to Pheebs's house, kick the door down, scream, and demand she tell them where I am. She won't have the answer, but they'll stop at nothing to track me down.

I will get off this plane to find the police waiting for me. I will get handcuffed and escorted to Dad's apartment in their patrol car, and I bet it won't be in the cool way—the sirens won't be turned on.

In Popo's wuxia dramas, when the disciple is dying, an immortal might descend from the heavens and help him, sometimes by giving him a bottle of . . .

ELIXIR!

It'd take a miracle for an immortal to show up now.

But it is pretty miraculous that Nor's being quiet. She hasn't even asked me about the beads of cold sweat dotting my forehead and temples. But then I see that the veins on Nor's hands have popped out. That's how hard she's gripping the armrests. I worry for their safety—they might be crushed into dust. She's also squeezing her eyes shut tightly like she's afraid the drop in altitude might pop her eyeballs out of their sockets. At this rate, she might end up pushing her eyeballs backward into her brain, and that's just gross.

"Nor, did your parents force you to go on this flight?"

She doesn't reply.

She must have had no idea that she'd be afraid of flying until she got on the flight. Sometimes you don't know how scary things are until it's already too late to back out.

I'll distract her from being afraid by saying something really deep and intelligent. "My dog is a cat."

Her eyes flick open. "Huh?"

"I—I mean, my dog's name means 'cat.' My sis named him that because he's weird. For example, when she and I used to take Maomi to a fenced-in dog park, he didn't do anything but watch the other dogs play. My grandma suggested he'd be happier

exploring the forest tracks at the end of our street.
I volunteered for the job."

## I MISS MAOMI

Along the forest tracks, Maomi often stops.
And watches me walk on.

And watches.

And watches.

Until I give in and call him.

猫咪, 来!
(Maomi, come!)

猫咪,
你好乖啊!
(Maomi,
you're such a
good boy!)

Repeat.

"I never told my family about Maomi's weird habit," I say.

Nor's fingers relax. But out the window, Singapore's skyscrapers are just coming into view. I have to keep distracting her.

"My sister would say he's weird and we should return him to the breeder and get a regular dog." There is a series of bumps as the plane's wheels hit the tarmac. I raise my voice. "I hate when she says things like that because . . . because . . . I'm just like Maomi. Weird."

Nor opens her mouth to say something, but at that moment, the blue sky is replaced by gray tarmac and Captain Yap announces, "Welcome to Singapore. We've arrived ten minutes earlier than scheduled."

I want to laugh-cry. I've landed ahead of time, but it doesn't matter anymore. The adventure is over.

Nor looks out the window. The plane is still taxiing along the runway. She's still gripping the armrests. She probably won't truly relax until she has stepped off the plane.

"Nor, I haven't defeated Frog in the Well."

Her back straightens, but she doesn't look my way. "I don't do business with you."

"I need your help, Shifu."

She whirls around. "What did you say?"

"I need your help, Shifu."

She lets go of one armrest to cup her ear. "Come again?"

I know she heard me, but I'll do whatever it takes to distract her from her fear of flying.

I NEED YOUR WISDOM, SHIFU!

I really don't, of course.

She grins smugly. "Fine. Only 'cos great shifus don't abandon their disciples."

"Thank you."

"Thank you, Shi . . ."

I know what she wants me to say. "Thank you, Shirley."

She rolls her eyes. "Do you want my help or not?"

"Fine, fine. Thank you, SHIFU!"

"Good disciple. I'll help you defeat Frog in the Well. What does he want from you?"

"Revenge."

Nor gasps. "Did you wrong him?"

"It was really our principal who wronged him. I just didn't tell our principal the truth."

"Interesting."

"Listen, Nor. I have to tell you something . . ."

I'm sor—

I've got it!

I know how to defeat Frog in the Well!

Is it hacking into Frog in the Well's email to find out what he wants? I'll break into his account and find out his demands. First I'll have to take a class called Hacking for Kids.

Is it me transforming into a ninja? I'll climb onto the roof of his house. While he's asleep, I'll slip in and drop a truth pill in his chocolate milk.

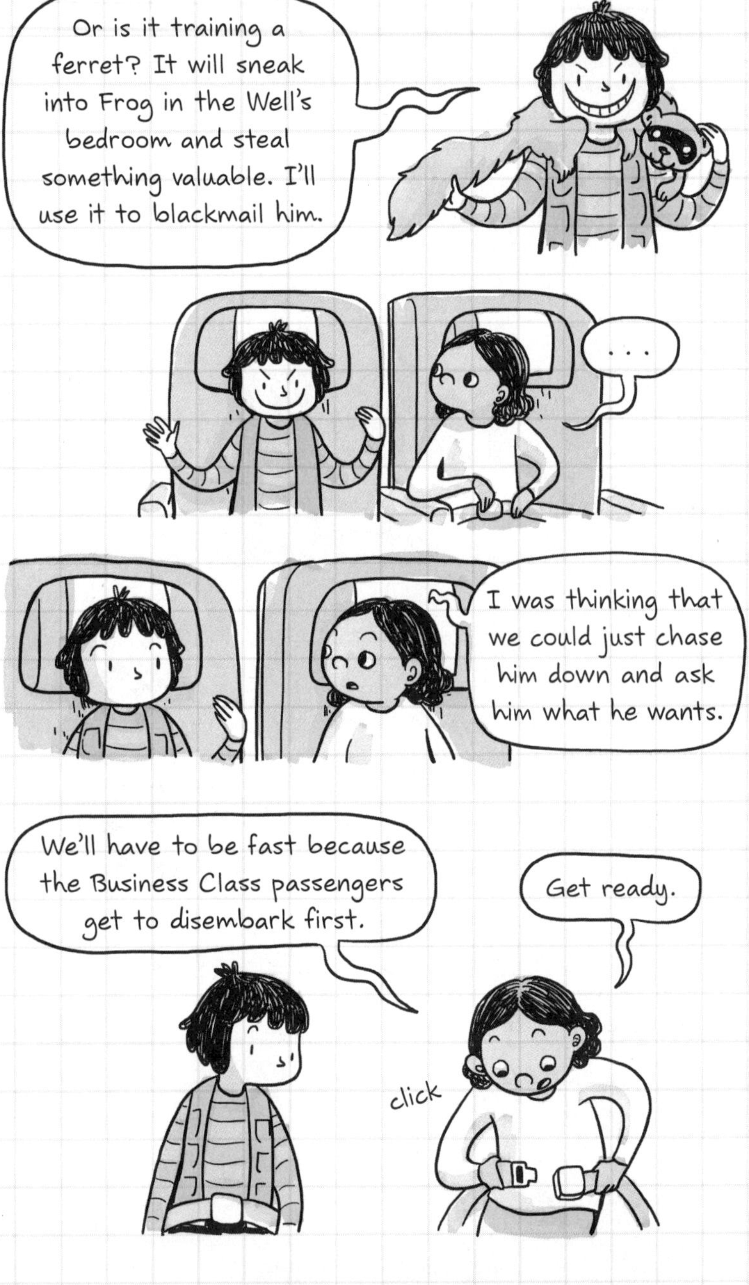

Or is it training a ferret? It will sneak into Frog in the Well's bedroom and steal something valuable. I'll use it to blackmail him.
. . .
I was thinking that we could just chase him down and ask him what he wants.
We'll have to be fast because the Business Class passengers get to disembark first.
Get ready.
click

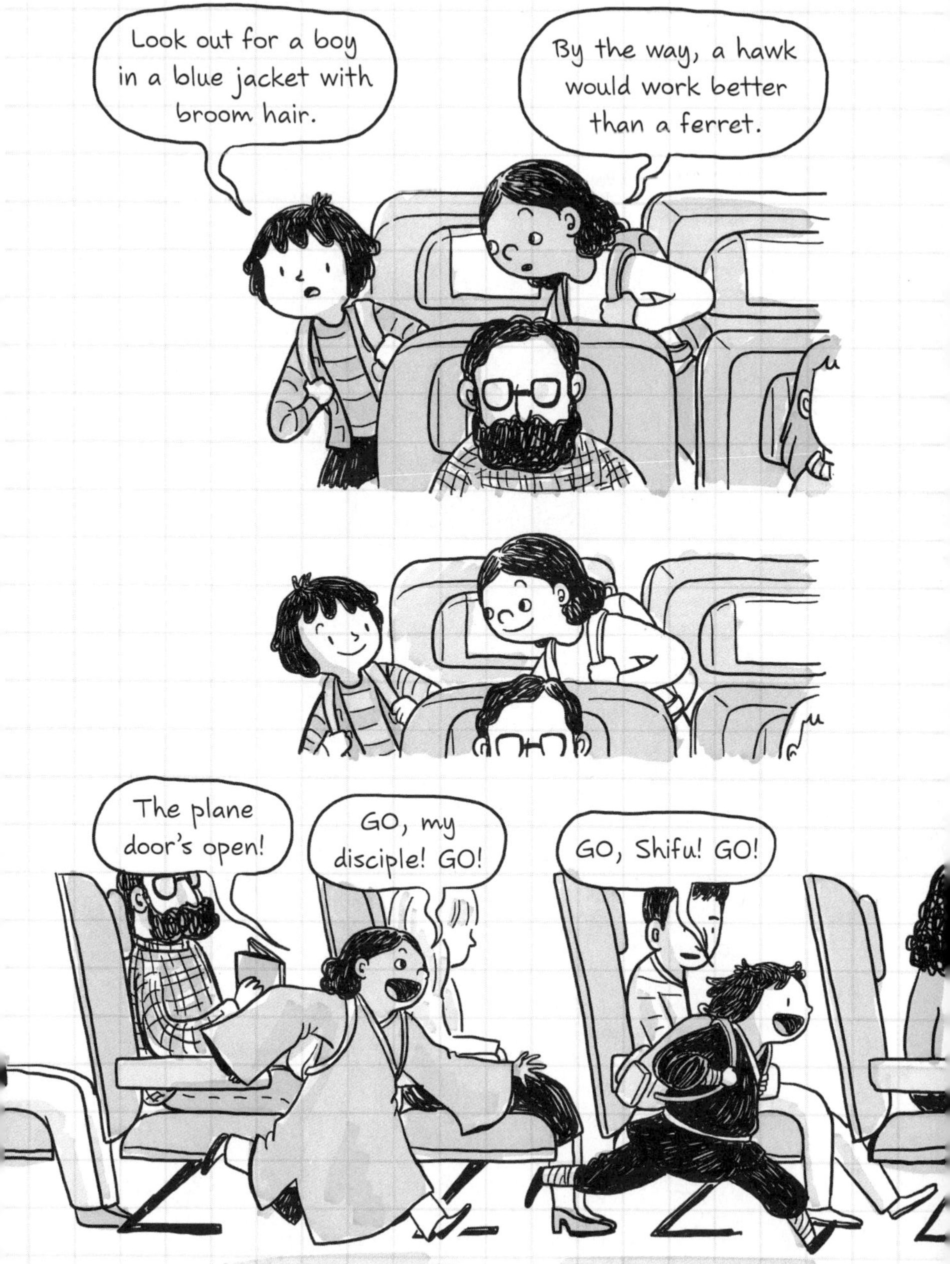

Look out for a boy in a blue jacket with broom hair.
By the way, a hawk would work better than a ferret.
The plane door's open!
GO, my disciple! GO!
GO, Shifu! GO!

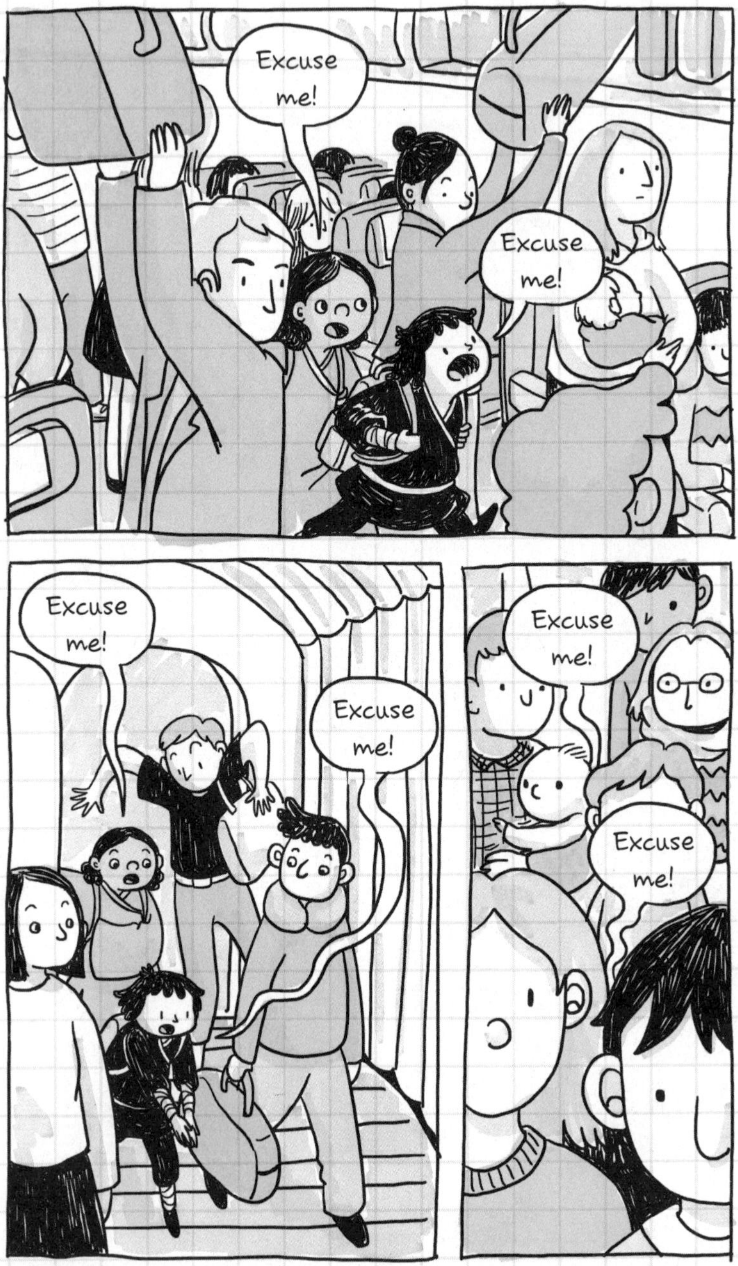
Excuse me!
Excuse me!
Excuse me!
Excuse me!
Excuse me!
Excuse me!

Frog in the Well is behind his parents, who are still on their phones.

As we're about to catch up to the Frog, I tell Nor, "Please stay ten feet away. Don't eavesdrop."

"You—"

"Private."

She crosses her arms and mutters, "More secrets."

She's annoyed at me again, but I don't want her to know about Fly on the Wall. Besides, like Popo said, at some point, a disciple must face his trials on his own.

I march toward the Frog.

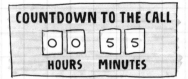

COUNTDOWN TO THE CALL

0 0 5 5

HOURS   MINUTES

Inside Singapore airport
FINAL SHOWDOWN! FLY ON THE WALL vs.
FROG IN THE WELL

In Popo's wuxia shows, the final showdown between the disciple and his nemesis usually takes place at a picturesque setting. A lush bamboo forest. A rocky cliff overlooking a serpentine river. A gilded hall of the royal palace. As I catch up to Frog in the Well in front of the bathroom, I call out.

HEY!

my secret manual, hidden under the evil mastermind's jacket

He looks surprised, but he doesn't stop walking. His eyes are on his parents, or rather, their backs. They haven't noticed that their son is about to face justice.

I could never have been an evil mastermind. If I were . . .

The sound of the Frog taking a photo brings me back to reality, where he is the true evil mastermind. As we silently follow his parents, he takes more photos. Of the ceiling. The window. The water fountain. SNAP! SNAP! SNAP! The same way he must have taken photographs of the pages of my secret manual.

Finally, the Frog's parents disappear into a sleeping lounge. The Frog turns to face me.

This is it. It's time.

The Frog stays silent, his eyes darting left and right. No doubt he's planning his next villain move. Before he can make it, though, I make mine. "I'll give you a hundred dollars to delete them."

He shrugs in a way that doesn't mean *I dunno*, but more like *what else you got?*

"One hundred and fifteen," I say.

"An hour."

"Huh?"

"I have to hang out here at Singapore airport for two hours before my connecting flight to New York leaves. I might as well go exploring with someone."

Those are the most words I've ever heard him speak. And yet I'm more confused than ever. A fly and a frog hanging out? The Frog is ridiculous level: Infinity. "I can't! I have to get to my dad's!"

Frog in the Well then disappears into the sleeping lounge after his parents, leaving me squashed.

COUNTDOWN TO THE CALL

0 0 5 2

HOURS   MINUTES

Heya there.
What's up?

"Shifu, I'm KO'ed. Frog in the Well says he wants me to hang out with him for an hour here."

"Is he that annoying that you can't hang out with him for an hour?"

"You don't know what he's like. He doesn't say anything."

My shifu mutters something.

"What did you say?"

"Kata periuk belanga hitam." She enunciates each

word this time. "That's Malay for pot calling the kettle black."

"What are you . . . All my family's pots and kettles are silver."

"It's an idiom!"

"This isn't the time to discuss idioms, don't you think? I can't spend an hour with the Frog. I need to get to my dad's—" That's when I realize that a SWAT team hasn't swooped in and arrested me. In fact, no one is even waiting for me.

I knew it.

Somewhere during the flight, the plane flew into a wormhole, and we've landed in an alternate universe.

There's only one way to test which universe we're in: Once I switch my phone off flight mode, if we're indeed still in that world where I'm a bao bao, my phone will explode with a million messages and missed calls from Mom and Jie, demanding to know where I really am and informing me that they've drawn up a schedule so that from now on, at least one of them will be with me every second of every day for the rest of my life and beyond.

I take my phone out and switch it off airplane mode. There's no connection.

Nor looks over my shoulder. "You didn't activate

international roaming, did you? Don't worry. The airport has free Wi-Fi."

"I know that." Because she just told me.

Strangely, my phone doesn't explode. To make sure we're still living in the same universe, I call Jie.

You'll be dead soon, Henry.

*gulps, sweats buckets*

WHERE ARE YOU? WAIT TILL MOM FINDS OUT!

You haven't told Mom?

WHERE ARE YOU?

I'm fine. Don't worry. I . . . umm . . . played paintball with some other classmates. But you haven't told Mom? Or anyone else?

PAINTBALL??!? YOU'LL BE BLACK AND BLUE ALL OVER!

How come you haven't told Mom?

Partly because of Pheebs. She has a good head on her. If she's covering for you, then whatever it is you're doing shouldn't be something too wild. Paintball is a silly reason but not unreasonable. But heck, Henry!

🐷 I'm fine! I swear!

🐨 Why did you lie? It'd better be a very good reason. I mostly haven't told Mom because I wanted to hear your reason first.

🐷 I lied because I'm never allowed to do anything.

🐨 Are you talking about flying to Singapore on your own to see Dad? That's an international flight. Of course we won't let you fly solo. You're twelve.

🐷 I'm sure I wouldn't have been allowed to go play paintball either. I mean, darn it, Jie! Mom won't even let me walk home from school on my own. It's only, like, five minutes away. And you drag me along when you go out with your friends, even though Popo can watch me. I just . . . I am not a baby.

🐨 Mom walks you home from school not just because she still thinks you're her baby.

🐷 Oh?

🐨 It's also because you've been acting really weird lately. I mean, weirder than usual.

🐷 I have?

🐨 You're mopey all the time. And you never tell us anything. Mom is, like, really worried about you.

🐷 What? I . . .

When we walk home together, all Mom ever asks

me are questions like *Have you eaten? What would you like me to cook? Are you hungry?* I'm sure she actually means those things, but maybe she's also really trying to find out other things, things a TV mom would ask. *How are you? How was your day? What happened?*

I have Mom, Popo, and Jie. They care for me.

That's why it's really not a big deal that Dad doesn't like me.

Henry? Are you okay?

I'm okay. I just needed some time to think. On my own.

I get that.

And Jie . . . I'd like another hour.

Hah! You're so funny sometimes.

I'm serious, Jie! Please please please please please pick me up from Pheebs's at 6 instead. My paintball friend's dad will drop me off there.

I give you an inch and you take a mile! I'm already doing you a big favor by not telling Mom.

🧑 Jie, you give me no choice but to do this . . . I know the reason you didn't want to go to Singapore this school break.

👩 Pft. Everyone knows my friend and I are going to visit universities—

🧑 Friend. You mean LOVER?

👩 * stunned silence *

🧑 * chuckles evilly * Pheebs said she saw you holding hands with a dude at the café.

👩 HOW DO YOU EVEN KNOW ABOUT THOSE THINGS?

🧑 I'm twelve, not ten. I won't tell Mom you're breaking her dating age rule if you pretend you never ran into Pheebs and buy me an hour.

👩 Henry, you're an evil mastermind.

**COUNTDOWN TO THE CALL**

| 0 | 1 | 3 | 8 |
|---|---|---|---|
| HOURS | | MINUTES | |

Once I'm done MUAHAHAHA-ing, I hang up and message Pheebs.

**PHEEBS**
WETALK

> Jie is going to pretend she never saw you. Please take care of Maomi for another hour. Jie will pick Maomi up from your place at 6.

Meanwhile, Nor makes a call. "Yeah, Dad," she says. "I just have to make my way to the immigration checkpoint, collect my suitcase, and then walk to the exit. Aunt Fatimah will be waiting there for me. Easy peasy."

The flight was fine. I wasn't scared at all.

. . .

There's nothing scary about the immigration and security checkpoints, but this is my millionth flight. It's Nor's first.

If I volunteer to escort Nor through the airport, she might get annoyed. Plus, she's still annoyed at me for not telling her everything about my feud with the Frog.

But it doesn't matter even if she thinks I'm her nemesis. I still want to help her. I'll have to come up with another idea to convince her to let me escort her.

The sleeping lounge has seats that are like pool chairs, but with thicker padding. The Frog's parents are lying on them. Not once have they taken their eyes off their phones.

In my family,
I'm the phone.

As I sigh
about my family
relentlessly pressing
all my buttons, the
Frog spots me.

I gulp. He clearly has something up his sleeve.

But I will not give up so easily. At the right
time, I will use a special wuxia skill called Killing Two
Eagles with One Arrow—snatching my secret manual
from under his jacket while simultaneously wiping
that smug look off his face.

"Time's up!" Nor shouts from outside the lounge.
"My aunt's waiting for me."

I turn to the Frog. "I agree to your terms on
one condition: Our first destination is the arrival hall."

He doesn't ask why. He just shrugs. I can deduce
two things from that gesture. One: Frog in the Well
might be an evil mastermind, but he's a surprisingly
flexible, easygoing one. Two: His evil scheme is not
time or location dependent. He could upload photos of
my secret manual from anywhere, at any time.

All it takes for him to destroy my life is a few
taps on his phone.

The Frog's phone and the rectangular shape under his jacket remind me that his thumb is on the nuclear button that could annihilate my world.

To Nor's credit, she does not mention anything about him being Frog in the Well, or that I'm trying to crush him. She even gets the Frog to say something: "Are you trying to avoid talking to him?" He points at me.

"I'm annoyed with him," she says. "Anyway, the

first thing you want to explore in this whole airport is the arrival hall? What's so amazing about it?"

The Frog glances at me.

I gulp.

He aims his phone at me.

I duck.

The Frog smirks.

I'd like to tape the corners of his mouth down, but I'd better not cross him. Besides, my phone goes BZZ!

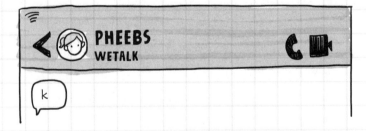

That's Pheebs's reply to my message that I need an extra hour.

k

That's all.

Pheebs still doesn't care where I am, what I'm doing. She's probably busy having fun with her new friends.

"What's wrong?" Nor asks.

"It's my friend. She's having fun . . . without me."

"You're still in my bad books, but we're having fun, too."

Suddenly, for the first time ever, I think about all those times that I was in Singapore while Pheebs was alone in Perth. Maybe Pheebs stared out her window, watching other kids play in the street. Maybe she had that big birthday party and started sitting at that table with more friends so she wouldn't have to spend another school break by herself.

But that shouldn't make her suddenly not like me and call me a helipad and The Odd Bunch behind my back.

There are so many other things I want to ask her. Has she always thought that I'm The Odd Bunch? Did she ever truly feel I was her sworn brother?

Her answers might hurt me, and I might never be brave enough to ask her those questions. But there's one thing I definitely have to say to her.

Which is the same thing I have to say to Nor.

"I'm sorry."

I repeat. "I'm sorry I told you to shut up."

She smiles. "I said mean things to you, too, so we're even. And I'm sorry I talk a lot. My mom and dad say I don't have a filter."

Filter. Like the water filtration system project I did in science class.

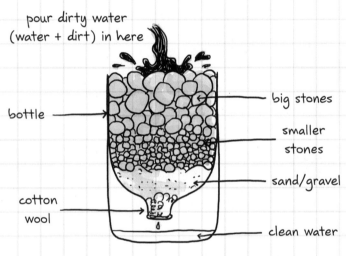

pour dirty water
(water + dirt) in here

bottle

big stones

smaller
stones

sand/gravel

cotton
wool

clean water

Maybe, unlike Nor, whose filter lets almost everything through, my filter is too fine. It doesn't let any dirt through. But it doesn't let any cool, clean water through either. And I'm left so very, very thirsty.

"And I was going to tell you this earlier, before Captain Yap interrupted me," Nor says. "Your dog *is* weird. Like owner, like dog." To me, weird usually equals bad, but Nor is smiling, so I guess she means it in a good way. Weird like the way Pop Rocks feel on your tongue. Weird like Maomi, a dog who likes onions so much he stole and gobbled up a plate of chopped ones even though onions are poisonous for dogs. Weird like a grandma who wants to ride a horse to walk the dog. "I'd like to meet Maomi one day."

"Only if Frog in the Well keeps his promise," I whisper. The Frog is several steps ahead of us, taking some pictures of the shops. "If he doesn't, my family will imprison me forever. No visitors allowed."

Nor whispers, "I'm going to tell you a secret."

"You have secrets? Impossible!"

She sticks her tongue out at me. "Just listen. My secret is that . . . dramatic pause . . ." She actually said *dramatic pause*. She's obviously weird too. "You're right. I am afraid of flying. I mean, even going on the Ferris wheel makes my palms all sweaty. My parents were worried I might be super anxious on the plane. It took some begging before they let me go."

"It's not that big a deal to be afraid of things."

But it is a big deal that she decided to fly even though she's scared of flying. To do something even though she's scared of it.

She does deserve to be my shifu.

"We can't go past this point," Tim says, taking a picture of the immigration checkpoint just ahead of us. "I gave my passport to my mom."

"Why didn't you get your passport from her?"
Nor asks. "You were the one who wanted to go the
arrival hall."

Tim turns to me.

"Umm . . . he's very forgetful," I say, before
whispering to Tim, "Would you wait for me here
while I take Nor there, Frog—Tim?"

Aha! I heard that!
I don't need you to do
that. I'm not a baby.

"I know," I say.

Oh . . .

Uh . . .

Yeah . . .

Uh-huh . . .

Actually, I have something to ask her. But what if she says no? After all, my friend-o-meter is out of order.

"Next!" the immigration officer says, and Nor walks toward the counter.

But I think about how brave Nor was, doing the very thing she was afraid of.

The immigration officer returns Nor's passport.

If I don't say it now, I won't have another chance.

She walks away from the checkpoint.

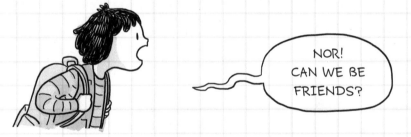

NOR! CAN WE BE FRIENDS?

Everyone's staring at me. And I'm embarrassed and I'm hopeful and I'm afraid.

She shakes her head. "WE ARE NOT FRIENDS! I'M YOUR SHIFU! AND I'LL MESSAGE YOU!" She must have messaged herself using my phone and gotten my number when she set up the free Wi-Fi for me.

She grins, waves, then skips toward the conveyor belts to collect her suitcase.

I turn and face Frog in the Well.

COUNTDOWN TO THE CALL

0 1 | 1 9

HOURS   MINUTES

small, driverless train

Fly on the Wall

Frog in the Well

The skytrain connects the four terminals of Singapore's airport. As the train zips down the rail line, I wonder where the Frog and I are going, why he wants me to tag along, what's in his head, which academy he trained at to be such a perfect villain. He's leading the way, so it's not that he needs me as a tour guide. He's still being the mouse, so it's not that he wants to engage in witty banter with me.

The skytrain pulls into Terminal 1. The Frog hops off. I trudge after him. We go up escalator after escalator.

BZZ!

Maybe Shifu is right. I shoot questions at the Frog.
"Why didn't you tell Principal Trang the truth about not

punching me? How did you know I was going to be on this flight? How did you convince your parents to take this flight? Why do you want me to hang out with you?"

I've figured out Frog in the Well's strategy. He's going to annoy me to death with the all-powerful Shrug 'n' Smirk.

He wanders around ahead of me, carefree and helicopter-free. Not once have his parents texted or called him. His parents let him go exploring with another twelve-year-old they've never even met. Just like that.

Now he's leading me out of a door to . . .

The moment we step into the Rooftop Cactus Garden, sweat starts pooling at my hairless underarms. My face and neck itch. In this humidity, each breath feels like I'm struggling with a stuffy nose. "Look, why do you need me—"

The Frog holds his phone close to a sign, and SNAP!

I study the sign. It explains the different types of cacti. The sign is in English and Mandarin. And the Mandarin word for cactus is:

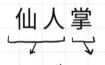

immortal's palm

This must be it. The immortals must have wanted me to come here, the Immortal's Palm Garden, to learn some deep wisdom that will fix everything, such as *it's what's on the inside that counts.* Which is especially relatable if you're a dog with worms in your belly.

This, the Immortal's Palm Garden, is the site of my final battle with my nemesis.

Our feud, and all my problems, shall end right here.

Either that, or my life's about to end.

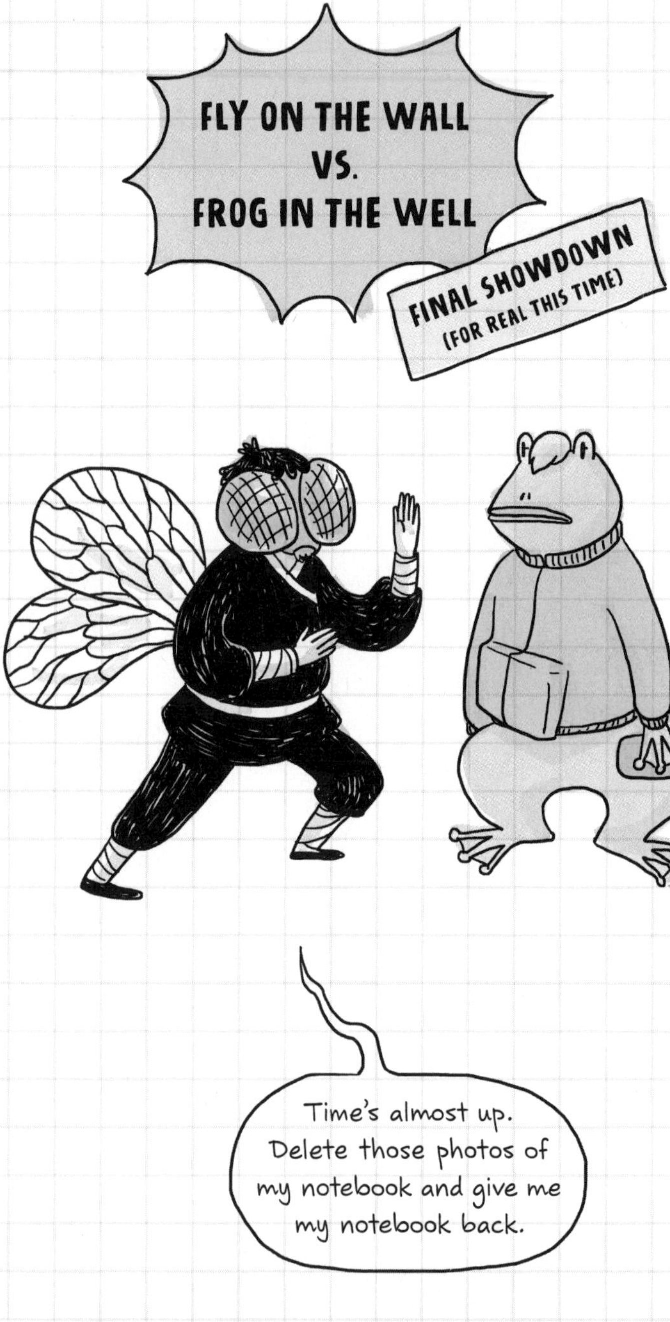
FLY ON THE WALL
VS.
FROG IN THE WELL
FINAL SHOWDOWN
(FOR REAL THIS TIME)
Time's almost up. Delete those photos of my notebook and give me my notebook back.

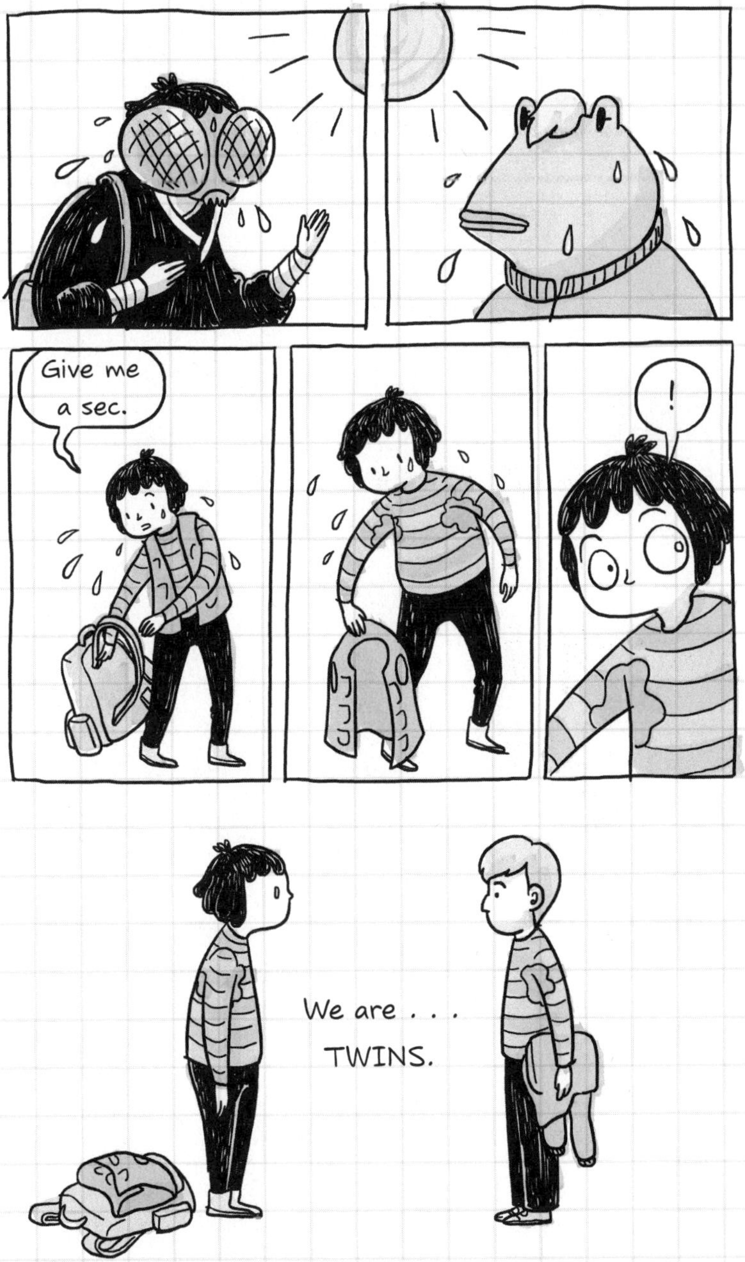
Give me a sec.
!
We are . . .
TWINS.

Instead of replying, "YES WAY!" the Frog
returns to his cactus photography.

I'm ready to chop down all the cacti in this
garden. "You told your parents one hour."

"My parents let me do whatever."

That must feel as good as leaping into a pool of
iced tea right now. "But still, you told them an hour.
They must be worried."

"I didn't tell them anything." He shrugs and
takes yet another photo of yet another cactus. And
another. And another.

With each SNAP! another puff of air is pumped
into the balloon that is me.

Puff. Puff. Puff.

My balloon gets
stretched thinner and
thinner. Through gritted
teeth, I say, "Tell me your
parents know where you are."

He shrugs. "They never know when I'm gone."

"You didn't tell them? What's wrong with you?" I'm shouting, but I'm not sure why. In my mind is an image of Mom pacing about with scrunched-up eyebrows after finding out that I'm missing. "They must be worried sick! Maybe they're calling the police right now."

"That's your family, not mine. I heard your family is what they call a helicopter family. Always hovering over you."

"You heard? From whom?"

The Frog shrugs. "Just around the school. You're not the only one who hears things . . . Fly."

The balloon finally goes POP!

What happens next, I have no control over.

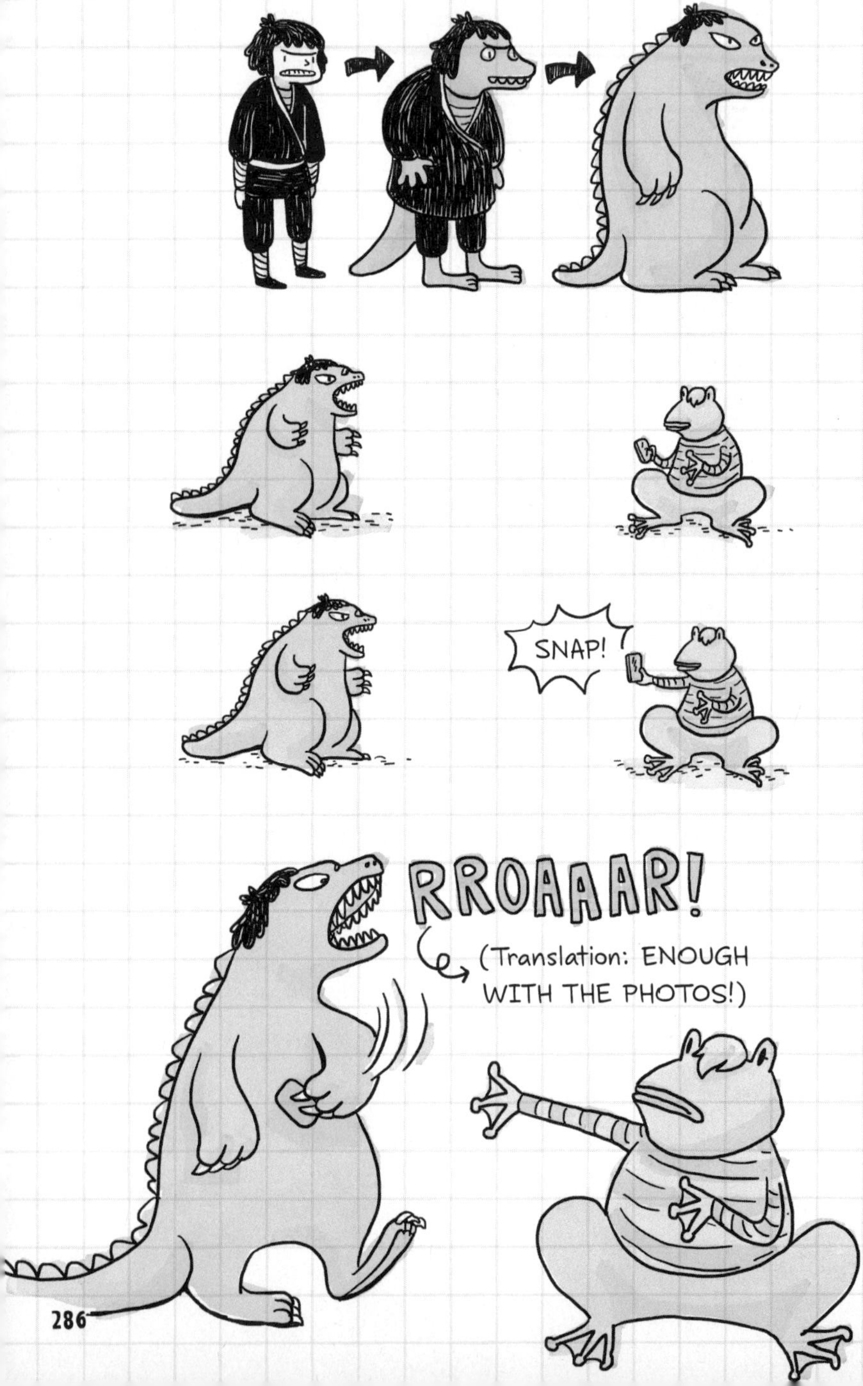
SNAP!
RROAAAR!
(Translation: ENOUGH WITH THE PHOTOS!)

GRR
GRRMMM
GRRRRR

(Translation: Cactus photo.
Another cactus photo.
Cactus. Cactus x 1,000.
Escalator. Fake flowers.
The water fountain.
Economy Class seat.
Airplane window.
Trolley of food . . .)

"Waitaminute," I say, "where are the photos of my secret manual? The evidence that I'm Fly on the Wall?"

Frog in the Well says, "I never said I had any."

I snatch his bundled-up jacket. My notebook falls out of it. "AHA!"

Waitaminute.
This isn't my
notebook.
It's a . . .

HI-YA!
comic book?

HI-YA!

For an evil mastermind, he's got great taste. But . . . "Where did you hide my notebook? Give it back!"

"I never had it."

"You said that you took it!"

He gives that smirk again. "I never said I took it. *You* did."

Sq—Squeak.

(Translation: WhWhat?)

I pick my jaw up off the floor. "But—waitaminute— why did you come into Economy Class?"

"To take pictures."

I realize: Tim likes to take pictures that are boring to me but interesting to him. He wasn't trying to spy on Fly on the Wall or steal the secret manual.

"If you're not Frog in the Well," I croak, "then who wants to catch Fly on the Wall?"

He smirks.

"AHA!" I point at his face. "You're lying! That smirk gave you away."

I'm not smirking.

There's a sesame seed stuck between my back teeth. I've been trying to use my tongue to get it out all day.

My brain would have exploded if it hadn't already done so just five seconds ago. "You didn't know I was Fly on the Wall until I just told you?"

"I always knew," Tim Aditya says. "I saw you making that post in the computer lab."

"Then why didn't you tell Principal Trang about it? Or tell him you didn't give me the black eye?"

"Same reason I didn't tell my parents where I am right now."

"Stop speaking in riddles. What do you mean?"

He studies a cactus, leaning so very close to it. He'd rather his eyeball become a porcupine than tell me any more. I have to seek wisdom elsewhere.

NOR
WETALK

Your advice stinks, Shifu. Talking doesn't work with Frog in the Well.

> You weren't such an easy nut to crack either, Disciple Henry. Anyway, you know why I told you about my secret? About flying?

> Why?

> Because you told me your secret about Maomi. I knew then that I could trust you with my secret.

I told Nor about Maomi to distract her from being scared during landing. I hadn't thought that it'd make her want to share secrets with me in return.

"Umm . . . Wanna know why I started *Fly on the Wall*?" I don't know if Tim Aditya reacts, because I look away. I don't want his pity. "It was because I was . . . maybe . . . lonely. My best friend wasn't my best friend anymore."

He doesn't say that I'll make more friends. He doesn't say, *Cheer up! The sun is shining! Tomorrow will be a better day!* In fact, he doesn't say anything. I can't help but look up. He's deep in thought. And at that moment, I don't mind hanging out with him that much.

I try again. "What about you? Why didn't you tell Principal Trang the truth?"

Tim Aditya leans closer to a cactus that's taller than we are. He looks like he's going to kiss that cactus and get very sore lips.

Thinking about kissing, a possible reason for everything pops into my head. It all makes sense now. How Tim didn't tattle to Principal Trang, how he wanted to spend an hour with me. "Look. I'm only twelve and don't even have underarm hair yet. I'm sorry but I don't *like* like anyone in that way yet."

Oh no. I've broken his heart.

I'm a little offended he finds it not just LOL funny but ROFL funny.

"Oh-kay," I say. "You don't like like me. Why, then?"

Tim Aditya continues laughing for another two

minutes and nine seconds. Finally, he says, "You know how Principal Trang called my parents to meet him?"

I nod.

"They never showed up."

I think about Maomi, how he does that weird thing of stopping, then waiting for me to call him. I always figured Maomi was just being his weird self. But maybe he just wants to see if I'd notice if he was gone. And he's so, so happy when I do, as though I make him feel like he's the thing that matters most to me.

Tim is still staring at the cactus. Maybe he doesn't want to see me pity him either. I face another cactus, but secretly, I'm watching him from the corner of my eyes. "So the reason you didn't tell Principal Trang the truth, and why you sort of ran away from your parents now, is to get your parents' attention?"

So slightly I might have missed it, he nods. Tim's first nonshrug reaction.

"Aren't you angry that I made that post about you? Calling you a mouse?"

He shrugs.

"But . . . getting your parents' attention is more important than the school thinking you're a mouse?"

He shrugs.

"Because . . ." And then it hits me: It's the same reason I didn't care that some of the comments on the blog called me names. "Because at least Fly on the Wall notices you. You exist."

He neither nods nor shrugs. He says, "Fly on the Wall is a jerk, though."

I look down.

Even with these brand new *in* clothes, I'm still the same old Henry who started the gossip and rumors blog. I'm still the Henry who told everyone in school his best friend is a backstabber. I'm still the Henry who doesn't dare own up to his mistakes. It was mean of Pheebs to tell Dee that I was a helipad and The Odd Bunch, but what I did was . . . babyish. That comics blog hurt Pheebs and Tim and so many other people.

I say,

"I'm sorry."

COUNTDOWN TO THE CALL

| 0 | 0 | 4 | 0 |

**HOURS     MINUTES**

Tim and I become BFFs and walk off into the sunset together.

As if.

But we're not nemeses anymore, and that's something.

We're also done having heart-to-heart talks. In fact, we pretty much don't say another word to each other as I lead him down the escalators and aboard the skytrain. When we reach the sleeping lounge, Tim's parents are exactly where we left them. They don't even look up from their phones.

Maybe Tim doesn't have the whole pool to himself. His mom and dad are in it, too.

I'd like my family to give me space like that sometimes, maybe more often than sometimes, but not all the time for forever. It'd get lonely. Just like how being a fly on the wall in school got lonely.

As for Tim, his parents don't seem to notice he's in the pool. They won't realize if he gets tired of treading water.

I turn to Tim and ask, "If this wasn't a big plan for you to take revenge on me, then why did you get on the same flight as me?"

He laughs. A regular laugh. Not a gloating MUAHAHA or a suspicious heh heh heh. "Did you actually think I arranged for my parents and me to be on the same flight as you just to take revenge? I wish I were that good an evil mastermind."

"E-evil mastermind?"

"Yeah. Like in *HI-YA!*"

If I'd known all along that he reads the same comic I do, we might have spent our recesses and lunch breaks discussing the latest issue or just reading separately together. I think Tim is like a durian.

fruit that looks like a lump of puke and smells funky BUT TASTES DELICIOUS

Life is like trying new foods. Sometimes you'll end up eating something disgusting, like anything pickled. But if you don't try new things, you miss out on the delicious foods too.

"I overheard my parents," Tim says. "They only chose this flight because it's half off on sale or something."

Tim's parents are Generation X-tra Stingy. Like Mom. Except Tim's mom's "cheap" is still my mom's "expensive."

Except my mom came to school immediately when Principal Trang called.

Except my mom always knows when I'm gone.

I hold my phone out to Tim. "What's your phone number?"

He looks at me suspiciously. "Why? So you can spy on me and threaten me into not telling anyone you're Fly on the Wall? You don't have to worry about that. I'm not going to."

"Thanks, but I'm asking for . . . Just in case you go on adventures on your own and really get lost. My family has helicopters. We'll look for you."

He snorts. As he punches his number into my phone, he keeps glancing up at me like I'm being The Odd Bunch. But he's The Odd Bunch too, so I don't actually feel so odd.

"Fly on the Wall is a jerk," he says. "You made me get detention. One time, I forgot all about it and Principal Trang called my house to make sure I was all right."

"I'm really sorry. But to be fair, I didn't stop you from telling Principal Trang the truth."

"Touché. It's not all your fault. Besides, detention's not that bad. I thought I'd have to study during that time, but mostly Principal Trang and I just sit in his office talking about sports or comics."

"Really?"

Tim nods. "But I'm not going to thank you for it."

"I'll try not to be a jerk anymore," I say, and he laughs.

In TV shows, this is probably where the characters hug, but I'm sweaty and Tim's sweaty and I'm not a hugger. Because my family is not a bunch of huggers.

My family is a bunch of *Have you eaten? Drink some cooling tea. Call me when you get there.* I used to think that those words would strangle me, but I guess sometimes they can be as warm as hugs.

"See you in school, Tim."

"See you, Henry."

I'm a few steps away when Tim calls out, "Hey!"

Then . . . who's Frog in the Well?

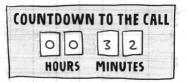

Hurrying to Singapore airport's exit

In one of Popo's wuxia dramas, the disciple lost a very important secret manual. He knew that 纸包不住火 (paper can't contain fire)—the truth always comes out—so he immediately confessed to his shifu. The disciple's punishment was to hold a horse stance in a dark cave for seven days and seven nights.

I open WeTalk.

> Pheebs, I have something to tell you . . . . I'm sorry, I'm sorry, I'm sorry. I'm Fly on the Wall. I made that post about you because I heard you tell Dee that I was a helipad and The Odd Bunch. I'm sorry. I'll do anything to make it up to you.

**SEND**

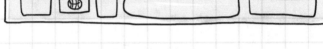

My thumb hovers over the SEND button.

The right thing is to come clean and apologize, but knowing what you should do doesn't make doing it any easier. That's why nobody flosses every day.

But I am brave enough to not be a jerk.

A minute later, my phone buzzes.

> I suspected, but ur drawing style was different N I just didn't believe u would do that. Guess I didn't really know you.

Being unliked by people stinks. But turns out, there are worse things.

Such as still wanting to be liked by the very people who don't like you.

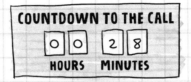

BZZ!

Disciple Henry, I'VE GOT IT! I downloaded the
HI-YA! game on my phone, and I figured out
how to get my character out of that room.
I thought that he had to search for some fruit
and turn into another animal. But turns out, it's
the opposite! He has to STOP eating the magic
fruit. He has to turn back into a person so he
has fingers that can grab the door handle and
open the door.

He has to be himself.

He has to be himself. Wise words from my shifu.
Being myself is being weird. Dad and Pheebs
don't like that.

But it's fine.
I'm fine.

I still have Popo, Mom, Jie, Maomi, and Nor. And maybe Tim. All is not lost yet. Pheebs said she's going to keep my secret. And the Frog hasn't revealed that I'm Fly. I still have time before I become extinct. I can still make The Call and declare my independence and enjoy my newfound freedom. Even if it's as short-lived as a slab of bacon placed on a kitchen counter within reach of a dog's slobbery tongue.

Ahead of me, there's a stationary shuttle. The driver is fiddling with his phone. I tuck mine back into my pocket. "Excuse me. May I get a ride?"

I'm going to make the countdown.

WOO-HOO!

Just got off the taxi

In the elevator of Dad's apartment building, going up

Almost time to declare my independence

DING!

17

knock
knock
knock

17B

17B

17B

No one's
home.

304

COUNTDOWN TO THE CALL
HOURS    MINUTES

I have to make The Call now, before Jie finds out
I'm not going to be at Pheebs's at six, before Mom
calls Jie to ask if I'm coming home soon, before any
of them calls me to find out where on earth I am.

But as I start to dial my home number, I realize I
can't make The Call. I don't have international roaming!

BZZ!

Waitaminute. How could I receive a WeTalk message?

Turns out, my phone has Wi-Fi! It has
automatically connected to Dad's wireless internet
because of the saved settings from my previous
stays. I think this counts as a miracle.

I open the miraculous message.

**POPO**
WETALK

Testing. Testing. I'm learning
how to text. Henry, let me know
if you receive this message.

I will let you know right now, Popo.

I open WeTalk and make a group call to Popo, Mom, and Jie.

Here we go. I'm going to declare my independence.

Henry, dinner is waiting for you.

你收到我的讯息吗? (Did you get my message?)

Uh . . . Henry?

You could have called our home landline, Henry. Popo and I are both home. But why did you call Jie? Aren't you with Jie?

Uh . . .

I'm . . .

in . . .

Singapore.

WHAT?!

HENRY! YOU SAID PAINTBALL!

You let your brother go to Singapore on his own?

I HAVE SOMETHING TO SAY.

Now is my moment.
After all that planning.
All that lying.
All that hiding.
All those truths.

DING!

Henry?

Dad.

17

金隆，你有什么话说，勇敢说。
(Henry, whatever you have to say, say it bravely.)

I want to say . . .
I, HENRY KHOO . . .

I'm . . .

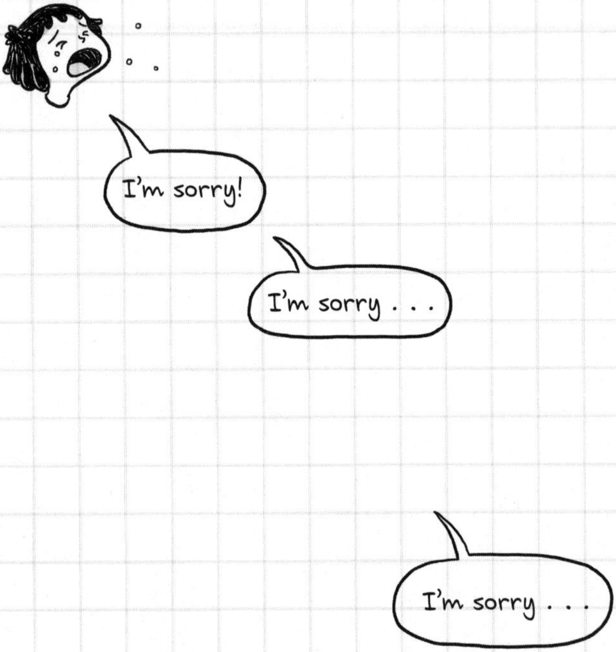
I'm sorry!
I'm sorry . . .
I'm sorry . . .

"I'm sorry I was born, Dad . . .

"I told myself I'm fine even though you don't like me.

But I am sad!
I am sad!"

Everyone falls silent. My cries sound even louder.

The first one
to speak is Dad.
Softly, so softly I
almost can't hear,
he says . . .

Why would
you say that?

"I heard you and Mom talking. When I was at
the doctor's. For the black eye," I say between
sniffles and hiccups. I can't see very well through
the waterfall in my eyes, but I think Dad looks
very, very surprised, so surprised that for once, it's
clearly written on his face.

He's silent for a moment, then he sighs. Not like a
sigh of relief, but like, *Oh, Henry, Henry.* "When your
principal called your mom to tell her you were hurt,
he didn't give any details, and she left me a voice mail
saying that she was rushing to school to take you to
the doctor's. I had no idea how badly you were hurt,
if you were going to be fine or . . . And at that time,
the thought of you getting hurt, or worse, was really
painful. For a selfish moment, I really did wish you
were never born. Just so I wouldn't have to feel that
pain. I don't know if you can understand that until
you have children of your own."

Sometimes people call their dogs their fur kids, and I think about how Maomi once spent two days at the vet hospital after he ate onions.

My insides hurt so bad then that for a second I wished we'd never gotten Maomi.

"I think maybe I get it, Dad."

Dad looks at me. Like, really looks at me. He looks surprised again, as if he doesn't recognize me. He mumbles to himself, "I didn't realize how tall you'd gotten . . ."

Since the last time I saw him, I've grown less than half an inch. He's trying to make me feel better. That means he probably likes me.

"You must have had quite the adventure," he said.

I have come to the end of my adventure. I realize there's no one thing, no magic elixir that will fix everything. The ultimate wisdom I learned is: There's no ultimate wisdom.

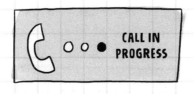

CALL IN
PROGRESS

THE EMOJIS THAT DESCRIBE ME RIGHT NOW

I'm not even sure why I can't pick just one emoji.
Maybe it's everything that has happened today.
Not just the bad things; the good things too. From
almost choking to death, almost killing a stranger,
being thanked for swapping seats, apologizing to
people I wronged, making a new friend or two,
losing an old friend. I've been riding a roller coaster
all day, and after all the bumps and drops and twists
and turns, now I'm puking all over the place.

Eventually, Popo, Mom, and Jie start talking
again. But I've used up all my words for the time
being, so they end up talking to one another for a
few minutes. I listen.

Turns out, Jie told Mom that my friends were

going to take cabs home, and as expected, Mom ordered her to drive them all home, thus buying me an hour. Jie figured that I hardly ever lie, and if I went to all this trouble, told all those lies, it must be really important to me. She also thought that if she helped me, I might start talking to her more often.

"Henry and I used to hang out together with Pheebs," she says. "Then her grades got terrible, and she had to spend all her time studying. He didn't want to hang out with just me. That's why I said I didn't trust him to stay home alone with Popo. But I sensed something was wrong even before that, around the time of Pheebs's birthday party. Maybe only I heard it, but right after the bicycle accident, he said he wished he had a different family."

Turns out, Mom heard me say that too. That's why she insisted on taking Popo's place on my walk home from school—she thought I might tell her what was bothering me.

I try to pay attention— really pay attention— to what my family is saying.

Don't cry, Henry. We'll all fly over tomorrow, and I'll cook you your favorite fried chicken wings.

Even though my family doesn't say words like *I love you, I'm proud of you, you're the best kid,* I guess those are the things they mean.

My family is not a TV Family. It's not Pheebs's family. It's . . . mine.

And now is my second chance to tell this family of mine that HENRY KHOO IS NOT A BABY ANYMORE!

I hesitate. My family's overprotectiveness is their way of showing they love me. I don't want to be a jerk to them, but I also don't want to be a baby forever.

You all don't have to fly over. I'll be fine staying in Singapore alone with Dad for the school break.
I want to.

"Oh!" Mom says. "I guess . . . If it's okay with Dad . . ."

"Okay with me," says Dad.

"I'll take care of Maomi," Jie says. "I'll even take him for walks in the forest. It'll give me a chance to spend more time with him before I leave for university."

"But . . ." I say, sniffling, "you always say you're sending him back to his breeders or dumping him at the pound."

"When I'm annoyed at him, yeah. But I don't mean it! I mean, I still wish he'd shed less and stop stealing food, but he's kinda grown on me. Besides, I can say whatever I want to him because he doesn't understand me unless it's *walk time* or *nom noms*.

At this point, I hear Maomi barking excitedly in the background.

"Thanks, Jie."

"Thank you for telling me to watch wuxia dramas with Popo! The one we're watching isn't bad at all! Turns out, the magistrate wasn't hunting the disciple at all! The shifu lied to spur the reluctant disciple to go on the journey to broaden his horizons."

Told you those dramas are great—

Wait.

A.

Minute.

I KNOW WHO FROG IN THE WELL IS!

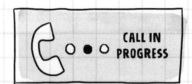

# BIG GIANT CLUES THAT ? IS FROG IN THE WELL

1. What Jie just said about the shifu lying to spur his disciple to leave and broaden his horizons.
2. Nor said that in Malay, the idiom is "frog under a coconut shell." I'm reminded now that "frog in the well" is not an English idiom! It's a Chinese one.

井底之蛙

well   bottom of   frog

3. Throughout the adventure, the true Frog in the Well kept feeding me a shifu's advice to their disciple, advice that encouraged me to go on.

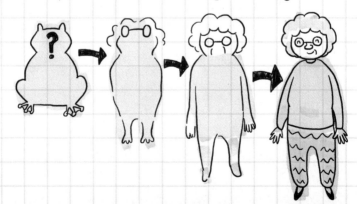

All along, I thought I was a fly on the wall who spied on everyone. Looks like Popo is the one who's a fly on the wall.

I was actually a frog in the well. Not *the* Frog, a frog. I was clueless about many things, but this adventure has made me jump out of the well and see how vast the sky really is.

I ask to speak to Popo in private. This time, Jie doesn't laugh that bao baos don't need privacy.

 婆婆，你怎么知道我是网上的墙壁苍蝇？
(Popo, how did you know I'm the Fly on the Wall on the internet?)

你姐姐教我怎样上网络时，她给我看墙壁苍蝇的博客。我知道你在儿童电子素描艺术班采用的画画风格。那时候我就怀疑你是那个苍蝇。后来我在看武侠剧时，看见你用客厅里的电脑写墙壁苍蝇的博客。(When your sister taught me all about the internet, she showed me Fly on the Wall's blog. I suspected you were that fly, because I know the drawing style you used for Digital Art for Kids. Later on, I was watching a wuxia drama when I saw you making a *Fly on the Wall* blog post on the computer in the living room.)

我还以为你对网络什么都不知道。我真是低估你了。那你也看到我在电脑买飞机票。你是不是一直知道我飞新加坡的计划? (I thought you didn't know anything about the internet. I totally underestimated you. You also saw me buying the airplane ticket on the computer. Have you known about my plan to fly to Singapore all along?)

 我可能知道的事 。。。你就别跟你妈妈提。 (About whether or not I always knew . . . Let's not bring up this matter in front of your mom.)

那我的秘笈呢? 你用什么高强武功来偷它? (What about my secret manual? What expert-level martial arts did you use to steal it?)

那真的与我无关。
(That really has nothing to do with me.)

我又不是神仙。
(I'm not an immortal, you know.)

The morning after the greatest adventure everrr
In my bedroom in Dad's apartment

I received an email last night, after I'd fallen asleep.

---

**SUBJECT**: Secret manual
[inbox]

**FROM**: norleenasalim@geemail.com
**TO**: henrykhoo@geemail.com

Hey Disciple Henry,

Soooooorry! I was the one who took your notebook. I was curious. You were keeping all these secrets from me, and I have this itch to know everything.

While you were in the bathroom, I took a peek at the book. The first page said: PRIVATE! KEEP OUT! You should know that made me want to read it even MORE! But then you came back, so I put it away before I had a chance to read it. And then you thought that Frog in the Well stole your notebook and you talked to me because you needed help, so I played along.

---

When I got home, I saw those words PRIVATE! KEEP OUT! again. MAN, I WANTED TO READ THAT BOOK!

Then I thought about how you have this thing for privacy, and how you told me a secret about Maomi later, and how nice you were.

In the end, I didn't read your secret manual.

Don't be too angry. I forgot to get your number, so if I hadn't taken your manual, I wouldn't have your email and wouldn't have been able to message you to give you advice when you were with Frog in the Well.

Anyway, if you tell me your address, I'll mail your notebook back to you. Or we could meet up sometime and I could pass it over and then maybe we could hang out. Maybe go to the zoo to see the orangutans. How long are you going to be in Singapore?

Bye!
Nor

P.S. If you don't want anyone reading your book, you should write on the front: PLEASE READ.

↩ REPLY     ↱ FORWARD

My secret identity as
Fly on the Wall is safe.
I got off scot-free.

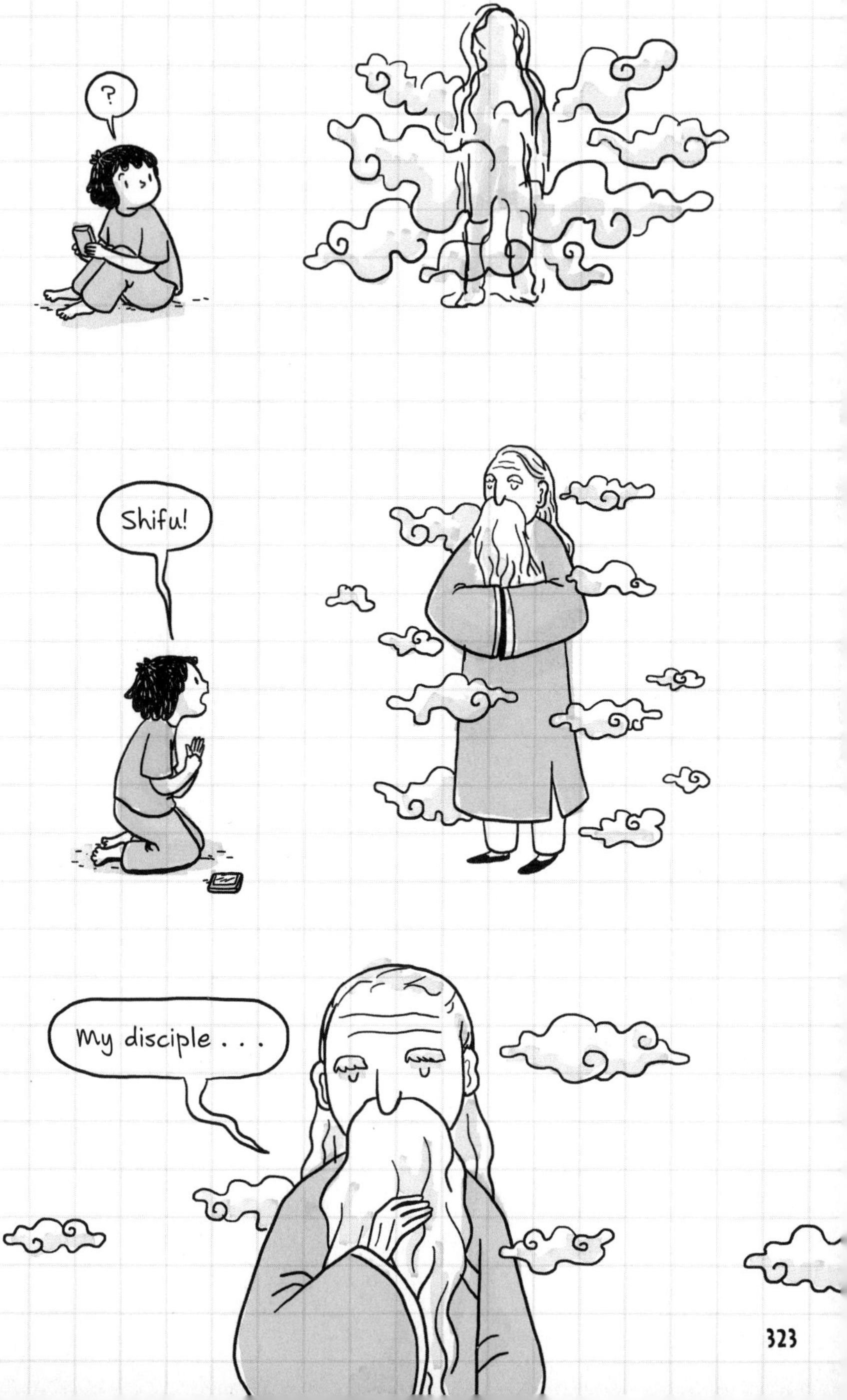
?
Shifu!
My disciple . . .

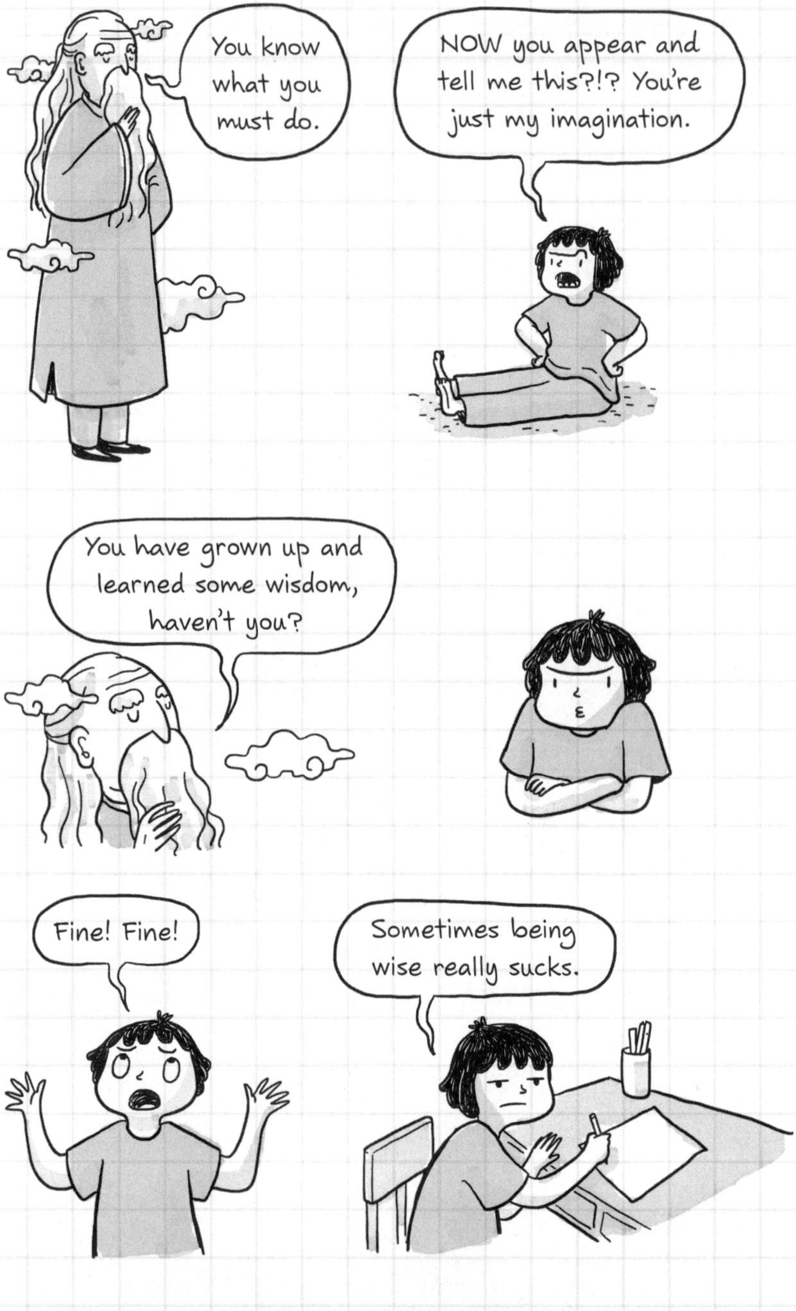
You know what you must do.
NOW you appear and tell me this?!? You're just my imagination.
You have grown up and learned some wisdom, haven't you?
Fine! Fine!
Sometimes being wise really sucks.

# FLY ON THE WALL

FLY
ON THE
WALL IS
FLYING
AWAY

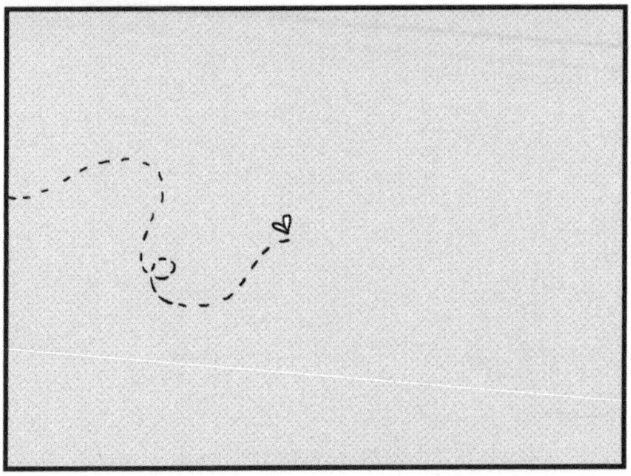

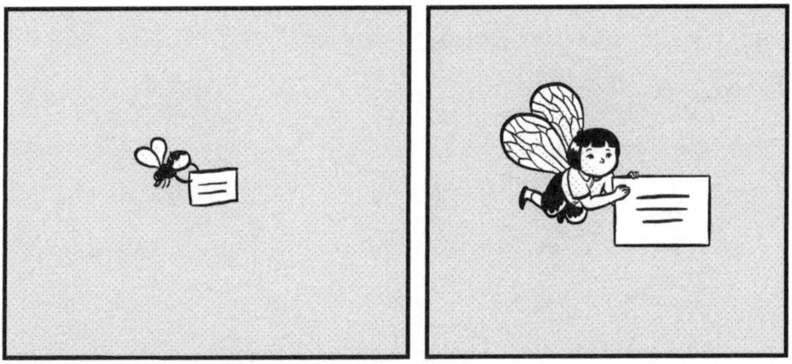

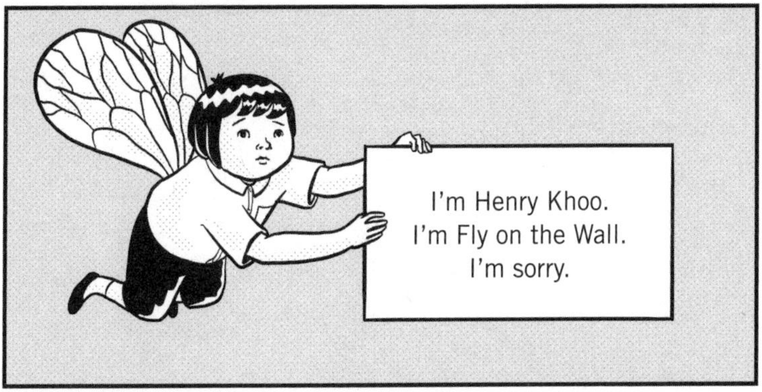
I'm Henry Khoo.
I'm Fly on the Wall.
I'm sorry.

Within an hour of posting that, there are already fifty-four comments: 60 percent of the commenters think I'm a turd, 5 percent think I'm a butt face, and 35 percent think I should draw more comics. I don't know if I will, but if I do, they won't be about rumors and gossip.

To be honest, I'm worried about how the students of Chatswood will treat me when I return to school. And Mom has forwarded me an email from Principal Trang, asking me to go to his office when I get back. *Rest assured, this matter will be dealt with to the satisfaction of all parties*, he wrote. I'm assured what's waiting for me is not a warm *welcome back* party.

I'm not looking forward to going back to school, although I know I have to. It stinks that I can no longer use being too young to know any better to get away with things.

BZZ!

It's an email from Pheebs.

FROM: pheebeee08@geemail.com
TO: henrykhoo@geemail.com

I tried to get u to talk to Dee and the others at that table because they're nice. I wanted them to see the parts of u they never saw. Like how funny n nice u are. N what an amazing imagination you have. But now I think u don't care about what they think of u. I wish I could be more like u in that way, but I care a lot about what they think of me. N I want to have many friends. And I thought u judged me for that. Especially when u stopped sitting at that table. I thought u hated me.

Later Dee asked me what I thought of u. I was afraid if I told her how nice n funny u are, she'd speak with u and u might say something bad about me. So I told her u were a helipad and The Odd Bunch.

I'm sorry.

I haven't talked to my dads about this, so don't mention it to them. They know something is up and they keep asking me to talk about it. But sometimes I just don't want to talk about things, u know? I'll probably tell them like next week or something.

P.S. I do honestly think u're kind of odd, but in a good way

⟵ **REPLY**    ⟶ **FORWARD**

I've been blaming Pheebs for feeding me fish but not teaching me how to fish. But it's not her job to teach me how to fish, and anyway, we're both still learning.

Pheebs and I probably can be friends again at some point, but not the same way we used to be. She'll never be my sworn sister again.

That stinks.

"Henry," Dad calls out from somewhere in the apartment. "Breakfast time!"

I'll cry about Pheebs later, maybe. It's time for breakfast.

As I enter the kitchen, Dad's phone rings.

"Hold on a minute, Henry, your jie's calling me to talk about her university applications." He steps into the living room, and I listen to him talk in multiple, long sentences about what Jie wants to do in life, her ambitions and goals.

Maybe Dad is just not so good at talking to kids. Maybe when I'm Jie's age, he'll be able to talk to me in multiple long sentences.

Five minutes later, he hangs up. "Your jie told me to remind you when it's time to shower. But I don't think that's necessary."

Now . . . breakfast . . .
How about kaya toast?

At this moment, I feel like a cup topped with just enough juice to be drunk without spilling, like a balloon filled with just enough air to float without drifting away, like a volcano surrounded by blue skies, no smoke in sight.

"Kaya toast sounds good, Dad," I say. "But let me make it for us."

HENRY KHOO'S BREAKFAST

extra
crusty crust

# ACKNOWLEDGMENTS

Jim McCarthy, who puts up with a lot: You have a cameo on page 255 (surprise!).

Brian Geffen, who puts up with too many fart jokes: Yessss! I got in one more fart joke in the dedication. Truth is, I'm not a big fan of potty humor either, but your disdain for it is too hilarious. Also, you're on page 101 and 255!

Jim and Brian: Without you two, this manuscript would have drowned in my river of tears. Thank you for believing in this book and me.

Carol Ly, who designed this book so beautifully: You're amazing! Also, you're on page 101!

MJ Robinson: Thank you for the gorgeous colors!

The INCREDIBLE Macmillan team: Kelsey Marrujo, Lucy Del Priore, Allegra Green, Melissa Zar, Ana Deboo, Melinda Ackell, Mandy Veloso, Mariel Dawson, Kristin Dulaney, Molly Ellis, Jon Yaged, Allison Verost, Katie Halata, Robert Brown, Liz Dresner, Rachel Murray, Christian Trimmer, and Jean Feiwel: Thank you soooo much for being so awesome.

Jin, Liping, Jolene, PY, YY, Joanna, Onglye, Chris: I love you all!

Jennifer Bee, Reese E., Bronwyn Clark, Fiona Stager, Genevieve Kruyssen, Mel Kroeger, Jo Noble, Pauline McLeod, Gail D. Villanueva, Jenny Stubbs, Steve Spargo, and Susan Chapman: Thank you for being with me on this journey and making it possible.

My dogs Poop-Roller (who is the inspiration behind Maomi) and Bossy Boots (who never gets featured in my books): Want to go for a walk? No rolling in poop, but.

# KAYA TOAST RECIPE

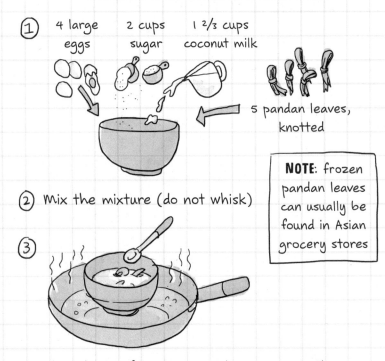

1. 4 large eggs    2 cups sugar    1 2/3 cups coconut milk

   5 pandan leaves, knotted

   **NOTE**: frozen pandan leaves can usually be found in Asian grocery stores

2. Mix the mixture (do not whisk)

3. 

Place bowl of mixture in a bain marie with simmering water for 1 hour until the mixture thickens into a smooth, cake-batter consistency. **VERY IMPORTANT**: Keep stirring the mixture or it will be lumpy. Take turns with your friends/family. (If it is slightly lumpy, push through a sieve.)

4. Let cool and serve.

   freshly toasted bread

   generous spread of kaya

   1/8" slices of cold, salted butter